THE WIDOW'S GAME

F.M. Lock

F.M. Lock is a practicing legal advocate who has successfully penned multiple psychological thrillers and crime novels, often drawing inspiration from the precise, high-stakes world of law.

He divides his time between two distinct lives and two continents: Wilmslow, Cheshire in the UK, where he lives with his family in a centuries-old, three-storey home overlooking a sweeping countryside view; and the bustling energy of Chicago, America. It is between these two worlds that he crafts his explosive thrillers and nuanced crime novels.

He firmly believes that the most dangerous secrets are always buried beneath the most pristine surfaces.

A Moment of Levity

Why did the thriller writer quit his job? Because he couldn't handle the plot twists in his paycheck.

What's a detective's favorite type of coffee? Decaf. They don't want any *grounds* for suspicion.

My neighbor told me he killed a man and buried him under the patio. I asked why he told me that. He said, "I thought you should know, since you're next door."

THE WIDOW'S GAME

First published in 2025 by MK Storyworks.

The paperback edition published in 2025 by MK Storyworks.

ISBN: 978-1-80700-037-0

TABLE OF CONTENTS

DEDICATION

For the secrets we keep.

AUTHOR'S NOTE

Every marriage has its secrets. Ours was no different.

Mine were just deadlier.

This is a story about the lies we tell to survive, the masks we wear to be loved, and the chilling truth that the most dangerous people are often the ones you trust with your life.

Thank you for reading. I hope it keeps you up all night.

—F.M. Lock

PROLOGUE

Some women collect recipes or porcelain dolls. I collect versions of myself.

The version I was with James: young, pliable, her laugh a little too loud, her eyes a little too wide. She learned to sail because he loved it, and she drowned with him on a lake so calm it looked like a sheet of polished slate. A tragic accident. The world sighed and moved on, and I pocketed the key to my first cage.

Then there was the version for David: sophisticated, slightly wounded, a bird with a carefully mended wing. She preferred quiet nights in, her trust a fortress with a single, well-guarded gate. That version was buried with him after a terribly violent break-in. Another tragedy. Another insurance payout. Another step up.

And now, this new iteration. The one standing in the kitchen of a multi-million pound house, the morning air so cold it bites the inside of my lungs. I didn't make the coffee. I didn't open the window. Mark is still asleep upstairs, believing he is the hero of this story.

Someone else was here.

My gaze falls to the crisp, white card centered perfectly on the virgin granite countertop. The words are simple, typed in a generic font, but they stop the very blood in my veins.

I know what you did to David.

Panic is a live wire, sizzling through my nerves. But it's instantly smothered by a colder, more familiar sensation: calculation. This was always a possibility. A variable in the equation. I pick up the card. The paper is cheap, the kind you could buy anywhere.

A strange calm settles over me, a blanket of ice smothering the fire.

They think they know me. They think I'm a victim, a pawn, a frightened woman waiting to be rescued.

They have no idea who they're playing with.

But they're about to find out.

Let the game begin.

CHAPTER 1
NOW

The first rule of building a new life is to destroy the old one, piece by piece. I learned that after James. And I've perfected it after David.

"You're quiet this morning." Mark's voice is warm, laced with the easy confidence of a man who believes he is the hero of the story. He slides a mug of coffee across the granite island towards me. The ceramic is warm against the cold granite. "Everything okay?"

I force a smile, the same one I practiced in the mirror for David. It's softer now, more genuine. He believes it's for him. "Just thinking about the boxes," I say, running a finger along the rim of the mug. "I swear they're multiplying in the night."

His laugh is too loud for the pristine, echoing space of our new kitchen. Our kitchen. The words still feel foreign. This house, with its floor-to-ceiling windows and silent, state-of-the-art appliances, is a world away from David's cluttered Victorian terrace. It is a world away from the metallic tang of fear and the persistent stain of red I spent all night scrubbing out of the oak floorboards in our old life. The memory, though still raw, already feels like a scene from a poorly lit film.

"We'll get it done," he says, his gaze dropping to my lips for a second too long. The hunger in his eyes is still there, the same raw, possessive hunger that started this whole thing. It used to make me feel powerful. Now, it just feels like a timer, counting down the seconds until he becomes a liability I can no longer afford to carry.

I take a sip of coffee. It's perfect, exactly how I like it. He remembers everything. That's what made him the perfect partner. Now, it's what makes him the perfect, meticulous threat to my freedom.

My phone buzzes on the counter. The vibration is a sudden, sharp intrusion. A number I don't recognize. The text is brief, professional, and terrifyingly direct. *Welcome to the neighborhood. We should talk. - Detective Rossi.*

The porcelain mug nearly slips from my hand. I catch it, but hot liquid sloshes over my wrist, a sharp, grounding pain that cuts through the adrenaline.

"You alright?" Mark is beside me in an instant, grabbing a paper towel. His touch is possessive, a comforting weight that I instantly resent.

"Fine. Just clumsy," I lie, meeting his concern with a tight wire of a voice. "It's from a realtor. Following up." Not a realtor. The police. The game is not just beginning; it is being run simultaneously by two players I hadn't even accounted for.

CHAPTER 2

THEN

The first time I saw Mark, I didn't see a man. I saw an opportunity.

He was standing by the coffee machine in the lobby of David's office building, looking gloriously out of place. Where David and his colleagues were all sharp suits and sharper angles, this man wore a faded band t-shirt under a blazer and had a dusting of sawdust on his trousers. He was talking to the building manager, gesturing with hands that looked like they knew how to build things, break things, fix things. My kind of hands.

I adjusted my grip on the folder of paperwork David had forgotten - his lunch, his dry-cleaning, his wife, all duties delegated to me - and calculated my trajectory. A slight stumble, a soft exhalation of manufactured distress, and the papers in my hand became a blizzard of white against the polished marble floor.

"Oh! How clumsy of me," I said, my voice a perfect blend of fluster and apology.

He was at my side in an instant, his movements quick and efficient. His scent, raw wood and fresh paint, was a welcome relief from the stale, expensive cologne David favored. "Let me help you with that."

As we knelt together, our fingers brushing as we gathered the scattered sheets, I let my mask slip for just a second. I let him see the quiet exhaustion in my eyes, the carefully concealed frustration of a woman playing a part she never auditioned for. I saw the moment it registered in his gaze - not pity, but a spark of dangerous recognition. He saw the woman behind the trophy.

"I'm Mark," he said, his voice lower than I'd expected. "I'm doing the fit-out for the new tenth-floor suite."

"Chloe," I replied, tucking a strand of hair behind my ear in a gesture I'd practiced to look both vulnerable and elegant. "David's wife. He's a partner here."

"Ah." A single syllable, loaded with understanding. The boss's wife. The unattainable. The ultimate challenge.

He finished stacking the papers and handed them to me. Our eyes held for a beat too long. It was all there, the entire unspoken contract, in that single look. His desire, my permission.

"I'm usually here around this time," I said, my voice barely a whisper. "David hates a cold lunch."

A slow smile spread across his face. It was a builder's smile, honest and rough. "I'm a big fan of a hot lunch myself."

It was crude. It was perfect.

Two days later, I was in his temporary office, a room that smelled of fresh paint and raw ambition. The door was closed. His mouth was on mine, and his hands, those capable, building hands, were mapping the territory my husband hadn't bothered to explore in years.

"This is insane," he breathed against my neck, his voice thick with a desire I had carefully orchestrated.

"I know," I whispered back, pouring just the right amount of terrified excitement into the words. "I feel like I'm standing at the edge of a cliff."

He pulled back, his hands cupping my face, forcing me to meet his desperate gaze. "You deserve so much more than this, Chloe. You deserve a man who sees you. A man who would burn the world down for you."

I looked up at him, letting a single, perfect tear trace a path down my cheek. "David would never let me go. He'd destroy me first. I don't know what to do."

Mark's jaw tightened. The hero complex I had been carefully stoking for weeks ignited behind his eyes. "No one gets to treat you like that. No one."

I rested my forehead against his chest, hiding my smile in his shirt. It was all going according to plan. He wasn't just my lover; he was my weapon. And I was loading the bullet, one whispered complaint, one staged tear, one calculated revelation at a time. He thought he was saving me. He had no idea he was signing his own death warrant.

CHAPTER 3

NOW

Detective Rossi does not ring the doorbell. She knocks. Three sharp, percussive raps that sound less like a request and more like a command. My heart performs a frantic, painful tap-dance against my ribs. I saw the unmarked car from the upstairs window five minutes ago, giving me just enough time to shove the blackmail note into the pages of a cookbook and school my face into a mask of polite confusion.

The adrenaline is a sour taste on my tongue.

I open the door. "Yes?"

The woman on my porch is shorter than I expected, with a sharp, intelligent face and dark hair pulled into a no-nonsense ponytail. Her eyes, the color of dark coffee, sweep over me, then past my shoulder, taking in the high ceiling, the stacked boxes, the pristine emptiness of the new house. This is not a social call; this is a professional assessment of the scene. She holds up a leather-wallet badge.

"Detective Maria Rossi. Homicide." She offers a thin, professional smile that doesn't touch her eyes. "Just doing some follow-up on the David Sterling case. You're Chloe Sterling?"

The use of my married name is a deliberate needle. A reminder of the life I'm trying to bury. I wrap my arms around myself, making my frame look smaller, more fragile. "It's just Chloe now," I say, a tremor in my voice. "And... I thought the case was closed. It was a break-in."

"It was," she says, her tone agreeable, almost soothing, but her eyes are still cataloging everything. She notices the fresh paint, the lack of pictures on the wall. "Routine procedure. May I come in?"

It's not really a question. I step back, granting permission with a quiet resignation. My mind races. Routine. Just routine. I repeat the words in my head like a mantra, trying to slow my breathing.

She walks in, her gaze lingering on a box marked "KITCHEN" that's sitting by the stairs. "Moving is stressful. Can't imagine doing it after... everything."

"It's a fresh start," I say, my voice soft, rehearsed. "That's what my therapist recommended."

"A fresh start. I like that." She stops in the middle of the living room, turning slowly to face me. She allows her eyes to sweep the vast space again. "It's a beautiful house. Quite a step up."

"The insurance," I say, the lie smooth and practiced. "It felt wrong to stay... there. Every corner held a memory."

"Of course." She nods, a gesture of perfect understanding that feels utterly false. "I just had a couple of quick questions. The initial report was a bit... sparse. You said you came home from your sister's and found him?"

"Yes." I look down at my hands, playing the part of the traumatized widow. "The door was open. The place was... ransacked."

"And you were at your sister's the entire night? From, let's see..." She pulls a small notebook from her pocket, though I doubt she needs it. She's testing me. "Seven p.m. until ten the next morning?"

A cold trickle of fear slides down my spine. She's checking my alibi with a forensic focus. "Yes. We had a movie night. She can vouch for me."

"I'm sure she can." Rossi smiles again. The mask is perfect, but I see the doubt in her eyes. "And the watch? Your husband's Rolex. The initial report listed it as missing, presumed taken by the intruder."

My blood runs cold. The watch. The one I planted in a dumpster in an alley two miles away. The one that was supposed to be found by now, solidifying the robbery-gone-wrong narrative.

"Yes," I whisper, barely audible. "It was his favorite."

"Strange, though," Rossi says, tilting her head, watching my face like a hawk. "It turned up this morning. A homeless man was trying to pawn it about two miles from your old apartment."

No. It was supposed to be found by now. In a different part of the city, not here. This is wrong. This feels like a move on a chessboard I didn't see coming. My heart hammers a panicked rhythm against my ribs.

I blink, letting a tear form. "I... I don't understand. Does that mean they caught the person who did this?"

She doesn't answer immediately, letting the silence stretch. "We're looking into it. But it is strange, isn't it? Why would an intruder steal a watch, then try to pawn it so close to the scene of the crime? Most thieves know better."

The implication hangs in the air like smoke. I force my breath to stay steady, my hands to remain still. "I wouldn't know how criminals think, Detective. I just want... I want this to be over."

"Of course you do." Her smile returns, but it's sharper now. "That's all I needed for today. But I'm sure we'll be in touch. This is my card." She slides a business card from her pocket and places it on the kitchen counter. "If you think of anything else. Anything at all."

I nod, mute, my throat tight.

She walks to the door, pauses with her hand on the handle. "One more thing. This Mark you're living with. How long have you known him?"

The question is a knife between my ribs. "We met a few months before David... before the incident. He's been a support. A friend."

"A friend." She repeats the word, her tone neutral, her eyes anything but. "That's good. Everyone needs support after a tragedy."

She leaves, pulling the door shut behind her with a quiet, controlled click. I stand frozen in the hallway, listening to her footsteps on the porch, the sound of her car door opening and closing, the engine starting.

Only when the sound fades completely do I allow myself to move. I walk to the kitchen, pick up her card, and stare at the name printed in bold, black letters.

Detective Maria Rossi. Homicide.

She knows. She doesn't have proof, but she knows. And now, the game has changed.

CHAPTER 4

THEN

T he watch is the key," I said, tracing the rim of my wine glass. The cheap wine felt appropriate for the cheap hotel room we'd been using for months, a stark, temporary bubble of desire and deceit. The air smelled of stale cigarettes and our own desperation. Mark paced, a caged animal fueled by lust and indignation, his anxiety heavy in the small space.

"It's too risky, Chloe. Planting evidence? That's premeditation," he insisted, running a trembling hand through his hair. "If we're doing this, it has to look like a random break-in. Something that got out of hand. We talked about this."

I gave him a look of gentle, wounded understanding. I needed him convinced that this wasn't murder, but defense. "I know. It's terrifying. But David is a creature of habit. He's meticulous. A random thief wouldn't just take the cash from his wallet and the TV. They'd take his prized possession. If his Rolex is gone, the police will never look beyond a robbery. They'll look for a desperate mugger, not a lover's quarrel."

I watched him process this, seeing the flicker of acceptance in his eyes. He relied entirely on my interpretation of events. I was always several steps ahead, framing the narrative for him just as I would for the police.

"He'll be at the conference in Leeds overnight. I'll be at my sister's, a perfect, grieving alibi." I lowered my voice, letting it break slightly, looking down at the stained carpet to conceal the satisfaction in my gaze. "You have the keycard I copied. You go in, create a mess, and... and you make it look like David came home unexpectedly and surprised you."

Mark stopped pacing and came to kneel in front of me, his eyes wide, earnest, desperate to cling to the fantasy. "I'm doing this for us. For you. He doesn't deserve you. The way he talks to you... the way he looks at you, like you're a piece of furniture."

His indignation was so genuine it was almost pathetic. I placed my hand over his, my touch meant to convey a courage I didn't feel, but a resolve I absolutely did. "I know. And after this, we can be together. No more hiding. No more lies."

It was the perfect lie, wrapped in the promise of a perfect future. He believed it. Of course he did. He saw himself as the knight, slaying the dragon to free the princess. He never stopped to consider that the princess might be the one who bred the dragon in the first place.

"We need to be specific about the mess," I continued, my voice steady and clear. "It has to look authentic. Drawers opened, papers scattered. But nothing truly valuable gone except the watch and maybe some cash. A thief interrupted. And Mark..." I paused, meeting his eyes directly, my expression grave. "If David comes home early, you have to be ready. He's physically strong. You'll need to defend yourself."

The knife was already hidden in my handbag, wrapped carefully in cloth. I would give it to him at the last moment, framing it as protection, as a contingency. He would never see it for what it really was - the murder weapon I was placing in his hands.

"I can handle it," Mark said, his jaw set with determination. "For you, I can handle anything."

I leaned forward and kissed him, soft and lingering, sealing the pact. When I pulled away, I let a single tear slide down my cheek. "Thank you. You're saving my life."

He believed every word. And in three days, David would be dead, Mark would be my accomplice, and I would be one step closer to the freedom I craved. The widow's game was elegant in its simplicity - the victim becomes the villain, the lover becomes the weapon, and I remain untouched, grieving in all the right ways.

Perfect.

CHAPTER 5

NOW

I delete the message and block the number, my movements swift and sure. The same way I deleted the security camera footage. The same way I planted the stolen watch in a dumpster two miles from our old apartment.

Mark buys the lie. He swallowed the performance whole. He sees what I want him to see: a beautiful, slightly fragile woman he rescued from a bad marriage. He has no idea that he's just another piece on my board, a temporary installation whose expiry date just moved up. He is so focused on the image of the hero that he is blind to the architecture of his own demise. He doesn't know about James. He doesn't know that the story I told him about David - the emotional abuse, the control - was a carefully crafted script designed to give him a righteous cause. And he definitely doesn't know about the note currently folded and hidden in the pocket of my robe.

I know what you did to David.

I look out the vast window at the manicured lawn, the high fence, the perfect, sterile safety of our new prison. The glass is cold and reflects my own strained expression. Who sent it? The detective? A witness we missed in our frantic clean-up? It doesn't matter. The first shot has been fired. They've made their move. And I am more than ready to make mine.

Mark is still pacing the short distance between the island and the refrigerator, rubbing the back of his neck nervously. His breathing is shallow and fast.

"You're sure it was just a realtor?" he asks, his voice betraying his lingering anxiety. He knows I delete calls and messages constantly, a habit I cultivated to protect my 'privacy' from David's 'control'.

"Yes, Mark. An aggressive one," I reply, my voice flat. "But that police woman... Rossi. She wasn't routine. She knew the watch had turned up. It was a test. She was watching my reaction when she told me." I turn to face him fully, letting my control assert itself over his rising fear. "Its location contradicts our story. It was supposed to be far away, lost in the system. But it turned up two miles from the apartment, in a pawn shop."

His eyes widen. The color drains completely from his face, leaving a sickly grey pallor. His hands are visibly trembling now, scraping his nails uselessly against the granite. "This is bad. This is really bad. Someone knew where I put it, Chloe. They found it, and they deliberately moved it closer to expose the lie." He grabs the back of a kitchen stool for support. "What did you tell her? Did you stick to the story?"

"The truth. That I was glad it was found," I say, watching him unravel, a clinical part of my mind noting the cracks in his resolve. He's the loose thread. He's always been the loose thread. "But it is a problem. Its location suggests the thief lived nearby, or that they abandoned it quickly." I offer no solution, only amplified pressure.

"What do we do?" he asks, his voice pitching higher in pure panic. He is a creature drowning in his own adrenaline, asking the puppet master for directions. I look at his frantic desperation. There is no we. There is my survival, and there are the obstacles in my way. He is rapidly becoming an obstacle. His mind is useless; the fear has claimed his capacity for logic.

"We do nothing," I say, my voice cold and authoritative. "We stick to the plan. We stay calm. We continue living our new life. And if they come back with more questions, we answer them the same way. You were a friend who helped me through a difficult time. Nothing more."

He nods frantically, grasping at the lifeline I've thrown him. But I can see it in his eyes - the doubt, the fear, the growing realization that this might not end the way he imagined. Good. Fear makes people predictable. And predictable people are easy to control.

For now.

CHAPTER 6

THEN

The lake was so still it looked like a sheet of polished slate, yet I knew the currents underneath were treacherous. James held out his hand, his smile easy and confident. "Come on, Chloe. Don't think about it. Just feel the boat. It's an extension of you."

I forced a nervous laugh, gripping the side of the small sailboat until my knuckles were white. "It feels more like it's trying to throw me into the water." The wood of the hull was rough against my palm.

"Then I'd just have to jump in and save you," he said, winking, the picture of the chivalrous, confident husband.

James. Always the hero. He saw life as a series of adventures to be conquered, with me as his beautiful, slightly fragile companion. He never understood that my fragility was a costume, one I wore because it was what he wanted. It was easier than showing him the steel beneath. That was the problem with James. He only saw the surface. He saw the calm lake, not the treacherous currents underneath.

A sudden gust of wind, timed perfectly with the slight adjustment I made to the sheet line, caught the sail. The boat lurched violently. James, caught off balance, stumbled. His foot slipped on the wet deck. For a breathtaking second, he was a puppet with its strings cut, arms flailing against the vast, indifferent sky.

Then, the sound. A sickening, dull crack as his head connected with the heavy, swinging boom, an impersonal, accidental violence. He didn't make a sound as he hit the water. He just vanished beneath the dark, placid surface.

I didn't scream. I didn't panic. I watched the spot where he disappeared, marking the time.

I counted.

One Mississippi. Two Mississippi.

The boat righted itself, bobbing gently as if nothing had happened. The world was silent, save for the quiet lapping of water against the hull. The lake looked exactly as it had a minute before. I looked at the spot where he had disappeared.

My heart was pounding, but my mind was preternaturally clear, calculating.

Fifteen Mississippi. Sixteen Mississippi.

The cold water would be a shock to his system. The head wound would disorient him. But he was strong, a good swimmer. He could surface. He could call for help.

Twenty-three Mississippi. Twenty-four Mississippi.

Or I could wait. I could wait just a little longer. Long enough for the cold and the confusion and the weight of his clothes to do what I couldn't bring myself to do with my own hands. I could give him a fighting chance and simply... not help. Not yet.

Thirty-one Mississippi. Thirty-two Mississippi.

This was the moment. This was the choice. I could dive in now, pull him up, call for help. Or I could wait. Just a few seconds more. Just long enough.

Forty-one Mississippi. Forty-two Mississippi.

I made my choice.

When I finally dove in, the water was shockingly cold, stealing my breath. I swam down, down into the dark, finding him suspended in the murky depths like a broken angel. I grabbed his shirt, his arm, anything I could reach, and pulled. He was so heavy, dragging me down with him. But I fought, kicking hard, breaking the surface with a gasp.

"James! James!" I screamed, genuine panic in my voice now, because it had to be genuine. "Help! Somebody help!"

I dragged him to the boat, heaved him partially onto the deck with strength I didn't know I had. I started CPR, my hands shaking, my movements frantic. Because I had to try. I had to be seen trying.

But I had waited. I had counted.

And by the time the other boats reached us, by the time the paramedics arrived, it was too late. James was gone. The grieving fiancée who had done everything she could, who had risked her own life trying to save him, collapsed on the dock, sobbing into the rough wood.

I was devastated. Traumatized. A victim of a terrible, tragic accident.

And I was free.

CHAPTER 7

NOW

Panic is for amateurs. It clouds judgment, shortens the breath, and leads to fatal mistakes. I learned that lesson on a still lake seven years ago, and I am learning it again now, standing in my silent, sun-drenched kitchen. Detective Rossi's visit and the recovered watch are not a catastrophe; they are data points. A shift in the variables. My initial plan accounted for human error, but not for a detective with the tenacity of a pit bull.

The original blueprint is no longer sufficient. A new strategy is required.

Mark is gone, chasing ghosts on the streets, a predictable reaction I can no longer afford to trust. His panic is a liability, a loud, flashing beacon drawing attention. I need to act alone. I need to find the source of the other threat - the blackmailer - before Rossi connects the dots between a suspicious break-in and a panicked lover.

The note. It's my only tangible clue. I retrieve it from the cookbook, handling it by the edges this time. The paper is standard, cheap printer stock. The font is ubiquitous. But the words... "I know what you did to David." Not "what happened to David." Not "the break-in." The phrasing is accusatory and specific. This isn't someone who suspects; this is someone who knows. Or someone who wants me to think they do.

I need to profile my enemy. I run through the possibilities, my mind a cold, logical engine:

1. A Witness: Someone who saw something the night of the murder. But Mark and I were meticulous. We chose a night with a predicted storm. The streets were empty; the sound of the rain was our accomplice.

2. An Associate of Mark's: Did he boast? Did he slip up in a moment of drunken pride? The thought sends a fresh wave of cold fury through me. His carelessness could be my undoing; he has always lacked my discipline.

3. Someone from my past: The list is short. My sister is too self-absorbed. My few friends from my life with David are inconsequential. James's family never liked me, but they live across the country and believed the sailing accident completely.

None of them fit the profile of a patient, quiet observer.

There is a fourth, more disturbing option. What if this isn't about David at all? What if it's about James? The idea is a lightning strike. It's been years. It's impossible. And yet... the note doesn't mention a break-in. It doesn't mention a robbery. It mentions what I did.

I walk to the large living room window, the note clutched in my hand. My reflection stares back - a beautiful woman in an expensive house, a picture of suburban tranquility. But behind the glass, my mind is working at a furious pace, calculating probabilities, mapping out contingencies.

The blackmailer wants money. They must. That's the only reason to send a note rather than go straight to the police. Which means they'll make contact again. They'll make demands. And when they do, I'll be ready.

But first, I need to find out who they are.

I pull out my phone and start making a list. Every person who could possibly know. Every loose end from the night of David's death. Every interaction, every witness, every face in the crowd at the funeral.

Someone knows. Someone saw. Someone is watching.

And I will find them before they find me.

CHAPTER 8

THEN

The storm arrived right on schedule. It wasn't just rain; it was a deluge, a frantic drumming against the windows of the apartment that mirrored the wild beat of Mark's heart. I, however, was perfectly calm. The script was written. The actors were in place. All that was left was the performance, and I was ready for my cue.

"It has to be now," Mark whispered, his face pale in the intermittent flashes of lightning. He was clutching the fireplace poker, the heavy metal cold and unfamiliar in his hands, his knuckles white with strain. "While the storm covers the sound. If anyone is out, they won't hear anything over this." He looked terrified, staring past me into the dark hallway.

I placed a steadying hand on his forearm, feeling the frantic tremor beneath the fabric of his jacket. "Just remember, it's a robbery. He's the intruder. You're defending yourself, defending me." I poured a lifetime of practiced fear into my eyes, forcing them wide. "He'll be so angry if he finds us here. He'll blame me for letting you in. He'll destroy me."

That did it. The last of his hesitation vanished, replaced by a rigid, terrified resolve. His desire to protect me - or rather, the version of me he believed in - overrode his moral compass. He nodded, a sharp, jerky movement.

I gave him the keycard. Our fingers brushed, his skin cold and clammy, a stark contrast to my own dry, steady hands. "I love you," I breathed, the lie tasting like victory and power. "Be quick. I'll wait here."

The moment the door clicked shut behind him, I moved. I didn't wait; I didn't hesitate. I went straight to the bedroom and pulled the old jewelry box from the top of my closet - the one that had been my grandmother's. It was wooden, heavy, and lacked any real monetary value, but David had always considered it a sentimental anchor for my 'fragile' past. I opened it, my movements efficient and emotionless. I took out a few inexpensive pieces, the ones David had given me, and scattered them haphazardly on the floor, mixing them with a few pieces of costume jewelry. Then I placed the heirloom box back on the shelf, untouched. A random thief wouldn't know its sentimental value. A random thief would have taken it. I needed to show not just chaos, but selective chaos.

From the living room, muffled by the storm and the intervening wall, I heard the first sound. It wasn't the crash we'd planned, the noise of a surprised intruder. It was the sickening, wet thud of metal meeting flesh and bone, followed by a guttural cry that was cut horrifyingly short.

The plan was in motion.

I waited, counting the seconds, listening to the muffled sounds of struggle, of a body hitting the floor, and then, the sound of glass shattering as Mark overturned a lamp in his panicked staging. My breath was even. My hands were steady. I focused entirely on the fact that I was one step closer to freedom.

Then, the apartment door opened and closed again. Mark stumbled into the doorway of the bedroom, his chest heaving. The poker hung from his hand, dripping onto the cream-colored carpet, a visual testament to his irreversible action. His clothes were disheveled, and a spray of blood, a small but unmistakable splash, marred his cheek. His eyes were wide and unseeing, staring into a trauma I could never truly understand, nor care to.

"It's done," he choked out, his voice a frantic whisper. "He... he came at me. I had to... I had to." He dropped the poker. It clattered against the floor, instantly silent against the noise of the rain.

I didn't look at the living room. I didn't need to. I walked to him and, with the corner of a towel I'd brought for this exact purpose, wiped the blood from his face. "You did what you had to do," I said, my voice low and soothing, a maternal caress designed to reassert my control. "You protected us. You protected yourself."

He grabbed me then, pulling me into a desperate embrace, his body shaking violently against mine. Over his shoulder, I could see the edge of the doorway, the mess beyond it. The scene was set. The performance was complete.

Now came the hardest part. The waiting. The grieving widow. The shocked discovery.

But first, I had to get Mark out of here. I had to clean him up, send him home, and make sure he would never, ever talk.

"Listen to me," I said, pulling back to look into his eyes. "You need to go home. Take the back stairs. Change your clothes. Burn them. Do you understand?"

He nodded, numb and obedient.

"And Mark?" I touched his face gently. "This never happened. We were never here. You were home all night. Do you understand?"

"Yes," he whispered. "Yes, I understand."

I watched him leave, slipping out into the storm like a ghost. Then I was alone with the silence and the rain and the body in the other room.

I allowed myself one minute. One minute to stand in the bedroom and feel the weight of what I had just done. Not guilt - I didn't feel that. But acknowledgment. David was dead. By my design, by Mark's hand.

Then I picked up my phone and dialed my sister.

"Emily? I'm leaving David's now. I'll be there in twenty minutes. Yes, I'm fine. See you soon."

I hung up. Looked at myself in the mirror. Smoothed my hair. Checked my story one more time in my mind.

Then I walked out the door, leaving it unlocked behind me, and drove through the storm to my sister's house.

In the morning, I would come home to tragedy. In the morning, I would be the widow.

Tonight, I was free.

CHAPTER 9

NOW

The digital world is both a shield and a sword. Within an hour of my post, the neighborhood forum is buzzing with sympathetic comments and offers of casseroles. The predictable hum of suburban concern is a soothing white noise, a sign that the local ecosystem is operating as expected. I scan the usernames, the profiles, looking for a crack, a hint of something darker beneath the pleasantries, dismissing the well-meaning, noisy majority.

And then I see it.

A reply from a user named Silent_Witness87. The name alone sends a jolt through me, a shock of pure adrenaline. Too on the nose to be a coincidence? Or a deliberate taunt, a bold assertion of presence?

The message is simple, devoid of the effusive empathy from the others, which is precisely why it stands out.

"Sorry to hear you're feeling unsafe. I live a few houses down. I often take late-night walks. I'll keep an eye on your property. You have a very distinctive garden ornament by the front door - the stone raven. Easy to spot. You shouldn't feel alone in this."

The air leaves my lungs. The adrenaline gives way to a cold, hard certainty.

The stone raven. It was a housewarming gift from Mark, a grotesque, gothic thing I'd shoved by the door to get it out of the way, hidden from casual view. It's not visible from the street. Not unless you've walked right up to the porch, onto the slate pathway. Right up to the door where the note was left.

Silent_Witness87.

This is them. It has to be. The level of detail is too specific, too intimate. They're announcing themselves, confirming their presence while maintaining the fiction of neighborly concern. It's elegant, actually. A public message that only I can decode.

I stare at the screen, my mind racing through the implications. They know where I live. They've been to my door. They're watching. And now they've revealed themselves, or at least, shown me the mask they want me to see.

My fingers hover over the keyboard. Do I respond? Do I acknowledge the message, potentially revealing that I've understood their game? Or do I ignore it, letting them think I'm oblivious?

I decide on a middle path. A response that's cautious but not suspicious.

"Thank you for the offer. That's very kind. I do feel better knowing there are vigilant neighbors around. The raven was a gift - I wasn't sure where to put it!"

I add a nervous-smiley emoji. The performance must be maintained.

I hit send and lean back in my chair, my heart pounding. The trap has worked. The blackmailer has stepped forward, thinking they're in control. But now I have something I didn't have before.

A username. A digital footprint. A trail to follow.

I open a new browser window and start searching. Silent_Witness87. Who are you?

The hunt has begun.

CHAPTER 10

THEN

The life insurance payout cleared with startling efficiency. $750,000. A tidy sum for a tragic, accidental death. I sat in the sterile, beige office of the financial advisor, a man named Mr. Albright whose smile didn't quite reach his eyes. He saw a young, grieving widow. I saw a gatekeeper to my freedom.

"Of course, the standard advice is to invest conservatively," he said, sliding a prospectus across the polished desk. "A mix of bonds and blue-chip stocks. Ensure a steady, long-term income."

I folded my hands in my lap, wearing the same simple black dress from the funeral. My eyes were dry. I had run out of tears for a man I never loved, years before the boat ever left the dock.

"James was always so cautious," I said, my voice a soft, sorrowful tremor. "I think... I think he would have wanted me to be bold. To use this as a true fresh start. Perhaps... real estate? Something tangible, something I can build."

Mr. Albright's eyebrows lifted slightly. He was used to widows seeking safety, not opportunity. "Real estate can be volatile, Mrs. Sterling. It requires a strong stomach."

"I have a strong stomach," I replied, meeting his eyes with a quiet, steely resolve that was genuine. "James taught me to face fear head-on. To see challenges as adventures." A beautiful lie. James had taught me nothing except the precise mechanics of staged accidents.

He studied me for a moment, reassessing. Then he nodded slowly. "Very well. I can connect you with some reputable property developers. But Mrs. Sterling, I must caution - "

"I understand the risks," I interrupted gently. "But risk is just another word for opportunity, isn't it?"

I left his office with a portfolio of investment properties and a network of contacts. The money from James's death would become the foundation of a new life. I was no longer the fragile fiancée. I was a woman of independent means, moving through the world with purpose and freedom.

The guilt that normal people might feel? The remorse? It simply wasn't there. I searched for it in the quiet moments, wondering if I was broken in some fundamental way. But all I found was satisfaction. I had solved a problem. I had escaped a cage. And I had profited from it.

Three months later, I met David at a fundraiser. He was everything James wasn't - controlled, ambitious, sophisticated. For a while, I thought I could stop. I thought I could play the role of the successful, beautiful woman and let it be enough.

But people are predators or prey. Controllers or controlled. And I had tasted freedom. I had learned that the only true safety comes from eliminating threats before they become problems.

David would eventually become a problem. They always did.

But that was a lesson for another day. For now, I had money, freedom, and the intoxicating knowledge that I could do it again if I needed to.

And I would need to.

CHAPTER 11

NOW

Mark's paranoia has begun to fester, turning from a nervous energy into something darker, more aggressive. The man who once saw himself as my savior now paces the confines of our new home like a caged animal, his eyes darting to every window, every flicker of shadow. The failure of his mission downtown to find information about the watch's movement has eroded his confidence, leaving only raw, exposed nerve.

He finds me in the living room, staring at my laptop screen, at the hauntingly simple username: Silent_Witness87.

"What are you looking at?" he demands, his voice rough with suspicion and lack of sleep. He comes to stand behind me, his presence looming and suffocating. I can smell the stale adrenaline on him, the scent of a man rapidly decomposing under pressure.

I don't close the laptop. I let him see the community forum, the thread I started. Let him understand the new level of threat, the sophistication of our enemy. "The neighborhood forum. I posted about feeling unsafe."

He scoffs, a harsh, ugly sound. "You did what? Why would you draw attention to us like that? We need to be invisible, Chloe! You're making us a target!"

"Because the police are already at our door, Mark," I say, my voice dangerously calm, the low tone forcing him to listen. I twist in my chair to look up at him. "The watch showed up. Rossi is sniffing around. Doing nothing is no longer an option. We need to control the narrative, or someone else will. That is the fundamental rule of the game."

He leans over, planting his hands on the desk on either side of my laptop, caging me in. His eyes are bloodshot and wild. "Control the narrative? This isn't one of your little scripts, Chloe. This is real. That detective... she's not stupid. And now you've invited the whole damn neighborhood to watch us? You're jeopardizing everything!"

"I've invited the blackmailer to reveal himself," I counter, my gaze steady, refusing to be intimidated. I tap the screen, pointing to the key reply. "And I think I have. This user, 'Silent_Witness.' They mentioned the stone raven by our door. You can't see it from the street. They've been right here."

The information hits him like a physical blow. He straightens up, the anger momentarily replaced by a dawning, sickly fear. He looks towards the front door as if he can see through the wood to the grotesque garden ornament beyond. "They're here? They live here? Watching?"

' It would seem so."

' My God." He runs both hands through his hair, pulling at the roots with desperation. "We're not safe anywhere. We're not safe in our own home." He begins to pace again, a tight, frantic path in front of the fireplace, his movements mirroring the trapped creature he's become.

I watch him unravel with clinical detachment. This is the moment. The moment where he becomes more of a problem than an asset. His panic is contagious, his lack of control a glaring red flag to anyone watching - including Detective Rossi, including Silent_Witness87.

' Mark," I say quietly, standing and moving towards him. "I need you to calm down. I need you to think clearly."

"Calm down?" He whirls on me, his face flushed with rage and fear. "How can I calm down? We killed a man, Chloe! We killed him! And now someone knows! They're watching us! The police are investigating! And you're playing games on the internet like this is some kind of - "

"Lower your voice," I snap, the command sharp enough to cut through his hysteria. "The walls are thin. The neighbors can hear."

That stops him. He stares at me, his chest heaving, realization dawning that even here, in our own home, we're not safe to speak freely. The paranoia settles deeper into his bones, and I can see it taking root, see it beginning to consume him.

Good. Fear makes people desperate. And desperate people make mistakes.

"We need a plan," he says finally, his voice dropping to a hoarse whisper. "A real plan. Not more games. Not more manipulation. We need to deal with this threat. Directly."

"What are you suggesting?" I ask, though I already know. I can see it in his eyes - the shift from panic to something darker, more primal. The cornered animal preparing to bite.

"We find out who this Silent_Witness is," he says, his voice gaining strength from the decision. "And we make sure they can't talk. Permanently."

There it is. The natural evolution of violence. One murder leading inevitably to the next. I should feel alarm, caution, the need to pull back. But all I feel is a cold, analytical satisfaction. He's offering to do exactly what needs to be done, taking the risk onto himself.

"That's dangerous," I say carefully. "If we're caught - "

"If we don't act, we're already caught," he interrupts. "This person, whoever they are, they have power over us. The only way to break that power is to eliminate the source."

I let the silence hang between us, let him think I'm considering his proposal when in reality, I'm calculating angles, probabilities, outcomes. If Mark eliminates the blackmailer, he becomes even more complicit, more bound to me. But he also becomes more unstable, more likely to crack under pressure.

Unless...

Unless he becomes the scapegoat. Unless both problems - the blackmailer and Mark's instability - can be solved with one carefully orchestrated move.

"Alright," I say finally, placing my hand on his arm. "But we do this carefully. Methodically. No mistakes this time."

He nods, relief flooding his features. He thinks we're in this together. He thinks I'm his partner.

He has no idea I'm already planning his exit.

CHAPTER 12

NOW

The lasagna sits on my kitchen counter like an unexploded bomb, its homely aroma of simmering tomatoes and sharp cheese a taunt.

The knock on the door the next morning is not the sharp rap of Detective Rossi, but a softer, more hesitant tap, immediately breaking my focus. I peer through the peephole, my body coiled like a spring. A woman stands there, holding a ceramic baking dish covered in foil. She has a kind, slightly nervous face, and her eyes dart around as if checking she has the right house. This is not the blackmailer. This is something else. A new, unknown piece on the board.

I smooth my hair and open the door with a carefully curated expression of polite surprise. "Hello?"

"Oh, hi! I'm so sorry to bother you," she says, offering a warm, slightly flustered smile. "I'm Sarah. I live just a few houses down on Elm Drive? I saw your post on the community forum last night and just felt so awful. I thought you could use some comfort food." She thrusts the dish towards me, an offering of suburban solidarity. "It's a lasagna."

The gesture is so normal, so achingly suburban, that it feels more alien and threatening than a direct accusation. My mind races, cross-referencing her with the forum usernames. She wasn't one of the commenters. Is this a cover? A way to get a look inside, to measure the distance between the blackmailer's digital reach and my physical reality?

"That's incredibly kind of you," I say, layering gratitude over my suspicion as I accept the heavy dish. "I'm Chloe. Please, come in for a moment. I was just making some tea. Let me put this down."

A flash of uncertainty crosses her face. She hadn't planned on being invited in. Good. That means the decision is now mine. 'Oh, no, I couldn't intrude..."

"Please, it's the least I can do," I insist, stepping back and swinging the door wider. An invitation is a test. I need to see her in my space, gauge her reactions. I need to know if this is genuine neighborly concern, or a casing operation.

She hesitates for a beat, then steps inside, her eyes doing a quick, unobtrusive sweep of the entryway. It's the natural curiosity of a new neighbor, but I scrutinize every flicker of her gaze. Does it linger too long on the security keypad? On the staircase? On the sheer emptiness of the hall?

"Your home is beautiful," she says, her voice echoing slightly in the sparse living room. "It's been empty for so long. It's nice to see it lived in."

"Thank you. We're still drowning in boxes, as you can see." I lead her to the kitchen and gesture for her to take a stool at the island. "It was just my husband and me, so it's too much space, really. It needs a family to fill it." I let my voice catch just slightly on the word 'husband,' watching her closely.

Her face immediately softens with practiced sympathy. "I was so sorry to hear about your loss. It must be so difficult, starting over in a new place on top of everything else. It takes immense strength."

The words are perfect. Too perfect? I turn my back to her to fill the kettle, using the reflection in the dark glass of the oven to watch her movements. She's looking around, but her posture is relaxed, her hands folded neatly on the counter. She seems entirely genuine. But then, so do I.

We make small talk about the neighborhood, the best grocery stores, the bin collection days. It's all so mundane, so boringly normal. And then, casually, as if it's an afterthought, she slips in the trigger. "You know, you're not the only one who's felt a bit uneasy lately. My motion-sensor light at the side of my house keeps going off in the middle of the night. My husband says it's a fox, but..."

She lets the sentence hang. The kettle clicks off. The silence in the kitchen is suddenly heavy, charged with a new significance.

' Maybe it is a fox," I say, my voice light as I pour the boiling water, masking the alarm bells ringing in my head. But my mind is screaming. The side of the house. The perfect approach to avoid the doorbell camera Mark insisted on installing. The perfect angle to see into our kitchen window, to leave a note on the counter.

Is she the Silent_Witness? Is this a veiled confession? A way to let me know she's watching, all while playing the part of the friendly, concerned neighbor? Or is she just a lonely woman making conversation?

I hand her a mug of tea, my smile perfectly in place. "It's probably nothing. But thank you for the warning. And truly, thank you for the lasagna. It was so thoughtful of you to think of me."

It's a dismissal, gently delivered. She takes the hint, finishing her tea quickly and making her way back to the door. "Anytime you need anything, Chloe, don't hesitate. We look out for our own here."

I watch her walk down the path, a normal woman in jeans and a sweater, and a chill settles deep in my bones. The threat is no longer a username on a screen. It has a face. It has a name. And it bakes lasagna.

I look down at the dish, the homely aroma now seeming sinister. Is Sarah my blackmailer? Or is she just another pawn used by someone else? Either way, the game has just become infinitely more personal, and a target has been identified.

CHAPTER 13

THEN

David believed he had rescued me.

We met three months after James's "tragic accident". I was the beautiful, sorrowful widow, a delicate bird with a broken wing, and he was the successful, stable man who could provide the gilded cage to heal in. He saw my grief not as a performance, but as a testament to my capacity for deep feeling. He never realized it was the aftermath of a perfect crime, the serene, silent wake of a carefully steered ship.

Our first date was at a quiet, expensive restaurant. I wore a simple black dress and let my eyes go wide and slightly lost when I talked about "trying to find my new normal".

"It takes incredible strength to carry on after a loss like that," he said, his hand covering mine on the table. His touch was possessive already, a claim staked on his new possession. "I admire you."

"I don't feel strong," I whispered, looking down at my wine glass, allowing my lip to tremble just so. "I feel... untethered. Lost without his anchor."

"Then let me be your anchor, Chloe," he said, his voice thick with the pride of a man who believed he was indispensable.

And so, I did. I let him anchor me to a life of quiet, suffocating control. He decided which restaurants we went to, which friends I could see, how I should dress for his work functions. At first, I told myself it was comfortable. Safe. After the chaos of staging James's death and the nerve-wracking wait for the insurance payout, David's predictable control felt like a respite.

But respites don't last. And control, once tasted, becomes addictive.

Six months into our marriage, David's "protection" had evolved into something darker. He checked my phone. He questioned my whereabouts. He made small, cutting comments about my appearance, my intelligence, my worth. He was systematically dismantling me, piece by piece, rebuilding me into the perfect, subservient wife.

The irony was exquisite. He thought he was in control. He thought I was his to shape and mold.

He had no idea that every criticism, every belittling comment, every act of control was being catalogued. Filed away. Added to the list of reasons why he, like James before him, would eventually have to go.

The difference was that this time, I wouldn't do it alone. This time, I would find someone else to pull the trigger. Someone who would believe he was saving me. Someone whose guilt and devotion would bind him to me far more effectively than love ever could.

I just needed to find the right person. Someone strong enough to do what needed to be done, but weak enough to be controlled.

I found him six months later, standing by a coffee machine, covered in sawdust and looking like he'd never met a woman like me in his life.

His name was Mark.

And he was perfect.

CHAPTER 14

NOW

The lasagna sits on my kitchen counter like a ticking clock, its homely aroma a taunt against the escalating paranoia.

Sarah's visit has shifted the entire landscape of the threat. A digital phantom is one thing; a flesh-and-blood woman with a kind smile and a direct line of sight to my house is another. I can't simply block her or delete her. She exists in the physical world, with all its messy, unpredictable variables.

Mark is no help. He's sequestered himself in his new office, a room he's barely used, supposedly working. But I can feel the thrum of his panic through the floorboards. He's a liability teetering on the edge, and Sarah's innocent casserole might just be the nudge that sends him over. I need to act, to regain control, and that means turning this new variable into an asset. I need to get inside Sarah's house. I need to see her life, to find her pressure points, to find the evidence she must be keeping.

The tool for this presents itself with perfect, mundane timing. The doorbell rings again in the late afternoon. This time, it's a delivery driver with a package for Sarah - a misdelivered parcel left on my porch by an overworked, indifferent courier. It's a box from an online bookstore, light and rectangular. A book. Fate, it seems, is offering me a key.

I don't immediately take it over. Instead, I wait an hour, letting the afternoon light soften into a golden haze. I change into softer, more approachable clothes - a simple cashmere sweater and jeans. I rehearse my lines in the mirror, softening my eyes, relaxing the set of my jaw. I am no longer the calculating widow; I am the grateful new neighbor, slightly lonely, seeking connection.

When I walk up her path, the parcel tucked under my arm, I make sure to notice the details my panic had blurred earlier. The well-tended flowerbeds, the child's bicycle leaning against the side of the house, the cheerful yellow door. It paints a picture of a normal, happy life. A life that could be a very convincing camouflage.

I ring the bell. Sarah answers, her expression shifting from surprise to a warm, welcoming smile when she sees the box. "Oh! My book! I was wondering where that had gotten to.

Thank you so much, Chloe. You really didn't have to go out of your way."

"It was no trouble at all," I say, handing it over. "It gave me an excuse to thank you properly for the lasagna. It was incredibly thoughtful." I let my gaze drift past her, into the hallway. It's cluttered with shoes and coats, a family home in active use. A small, framed photo on a console table shows her with a man I assume is her husband and a young girl of about eight. The perfect, all-American family. "What a beautiful home."

"It's a mess, is what it is," she laughs, but she seems genuinely pleased by the compliment. "Please, come in for a bit. I just put the kettle on. Let me get you a cup of tea."

The invitation is exactly what I need. I step inside, my eyes cataloguing everything even as I maintain the mask of grateful neighbor. The house is the opposite of mine - lived in, comfortable, cluttered with the debris of an ordinary life. Children's artwork on the fridge. A stack of bills on the counter. A dog bed in the corner, though no dog in sight.

But as Sarah leads me through to the kitchen, chattering about her daughter's school play and her husband's new job, I notice something that makes my pulse quicken.

On her desk in the corner, partially hidden beneath a pile of mail, is a laptop. The screen is dark, but beside it sits a small notebook. And peeking out from under that notebook is the corner of a photograph.

A photograph of my house.

My heart hammers, but my face remains serene. I accept the tea she offers, sit at her kitchen table, and make polite conversation about absolutely nothing. All the while, my mind is racing, calculating distances, sight lines, opportunities.

Sarah is the blackmailer. I'm certain now.

The only question is: what am I going to do about it?

CHAPTER 15

NOW

The binoculars.

The image of them, sleek and black and utterly out of place on Sarah's cluttered kitchen shelf, burns behind my eyes for the rest of the day. It rewrites every interaction, every kind word. The friendly neighbor is a lie. The lasagna was a Trojan horse. She wasn't just being nosy; she was conducting surveillance. The "motion-sensor light" going off? A test to see how I'd react to the idea of being watched. My post on the forum was a gift to her, an invitation to step out of the shadows and engage directly, all under the perfect cover of suburban concern.

I spend the evening performing normalcy for Mark, who picks at the lasagna I reheated, his silence a heavy, accusing thing. He doesn't ask about my visit to Sarah's. He's retreated so far into his own fear that he barely seems to see me at all, consumed by the ghosts of his own actions. This is a new problem. A disconnected, unpredictable Mark is even more dangerous than a panicked one. He is becoming a volatile bomb I need to disarm quickly.

"I'm going to take a bath," I announce, needing to escape the suffocating atmosphere of the kitchen and plan the necessary counter-attack.

He just grunts, not looking up from his plate, nodding his exhausted permission.

Upstairs, I don't run a bath. I stand in the dark of the bedroom, peering through a narrow gap in the blinds towards Sarah's house. Lights are on upstairs and down. The family is home. A part of me, the part that still remembers how to be human, tries to rationalize it. Her husband is a birdwatcher. She uses them for stargazing. But the professional in me, the killer, knows better. You don't hide bird-watching binoculars behind a cookie jar. You hide the tools of your trade.

I need proof. I need to know what she's seen, what she knows, and what she intends to do with that information. The blackmail note was just the opening gambit. There will be a demand. There is always a demand. I need to know the terms of the game before the ransom note arrives. I need leverage.

An hour later, the downstairs light in Sarah's house goes out. Then the upstairs one. The street falls into a deep, moon-washed silence. It's time.

I change into black leggings and a dark, long-sleeved top. I pull my hair into a tight bun. I don't need a torch; the ambient light from the streetlamps is enough for my eyes, which have been trained for low light. My heart is not pounding with fear, but with a cold, focused intensity. This is what I am good at. This is the core of who I am: movement in the shadows, the solving of problems.

I slip out the back door, locking it silently behind me, confirming my staged absence. The cool night air is a shock against my skin. I keep to the edge of our garden, using the tall, ornamental grasses as cover until I reach the fence that separates our property from Sarah's. It's a six-foot wooden panel. I find a foothold, hoist myself up, and drop soundlessly into her backyard.

It's a child's paradise. A small play-set, a scattered collection of plastic toys, a tiny fairy door nailed to the base of a large oak tree. The domesticity of it is a stark, jarring contrast to my mission. I push the sentiment aside. I can't afford sentimentality.

Her back door is locked, but the window above the kitchen sink is open a crack, just enough to let in the night air. A careless mistake. A fatal one for her. I find a small trowel left in a flowerbed and, working with painstaking slowness, use the handle to gently widen the gap, pushing the latch until it clicks open.

I'm inside.

The house is silent except for the hum of the refrigerator and the distant sound of someone snoring upstairs. I move through the kitchen like a ghost, my feet silent on the tile floor.

My eyes adjust to the deeper darkness of the interior, and I head straight for what I need: her laptop.

It's still on the counter where I saw it earlier. I open it carefully, the blue glow of the screen illuminating my face. It requires a password, of course. But Sarah strikes me as the type who prioritizes convenience over security. I try the obvious ones: her daughter's name, variations of her address, common passwords. Nothing.

Then I remember the photo on the console table. The daughter. Maddie. I try: Maddie2017. The year she would have been born based on her age.

The laptop unlocks.

I'm in.

CHAPTER 16

THEN

The human psyche is a fascinating, predictable machine.

Apply the right pressure, and it will crack along predetermined fault lines. With James, the pressure was his own ego and his profound need to be the hero on a grand adventure. He required a narrative where he was the central, powerful figure, and I simply adjusted the plot until his own confidence led to his tragic, fatal error. With David, it was his overwhelming need for absolute control and his secret, gnawing fear of being ordinary and unloved. The pressure I applied there was subtle - the slow erosion of his self-image by introducing the possibility of someone more capable.

With Mark, it was his white-knight complex, his deep-seated belief that he was rescuing a beautiful damsel in distress. The emotional architecture of his vulnerability was built on his need to feel necessary, to be the strong protector. All I had to do was present David as the dragon and myself as the prize. His psychology did the rest.

I studied him for weeks before making my move. I watched him in the building, noted his routines, his interactions. He was kind to the cleaning staff, patient with the flustered receptionist, and clearly took pride in his work. He was a good man. That was precisely why he was perfect. Good men believe in justice. Good men believe bad things happen to bad people and that they, through their own moral superiority, can set things right.

The first time we spoke - the staged paper-dropping incident - I made sure he saw exactly what I needed him to see. Not a manipulator, but a victim. Not a huntress, but prey.

Every subsequent interaction was calibrated. A bruise on my arm, carefully placed and artfully explained away. "I'm so clumsy." A phone call from David that I took in his presence, my voice becoming smaller, more apologetic. "Yes, of course. I'm sorry. I'll be home right away." The way I flinched when Mark raised his hand too quickly to gesture, then immediately apologized for my "silly" reaction.

He ate it up. Every morsel of manufactured vulnerability fed his growing rage against David and his deepening devotion to me. By the time I suggested - in the most tentative, frightened whisper - that David would never let me go, that he'd rather see me dead than divorced, Mark was already primed. He was ready to kill for me before I ever explicitly asked.

That's the beauty of psychological manipulation. You don't force people to do things. You create the conditions where they choose to do them, believing it was their idea all along.

I made Mark into a murderer. And he thanked me for the opportunity.

Now, I need to unmake him just as carefully. Because he's served his purpose, and in this game, pieces that have outlived their usefulness must be removed from the board.

The question is: how do I eliminate Mark without implicating myself?

The answer is becoming clearer with each passing hour. I don't eliminate him. I let someone else do it for me. Someone who's already hunting. Someone who already has evidence of our crime.

Sarah.

She's my weapon now. I just need to point her in the right direction.

CHAPTER 17

NOW

Planning Sarah's demise is a different calculus than the others. James was an opportunity. David was a project. Sarah is a clear and present danger. She is not a pawn; she is a player who has openly revealed her hand, and her hand holds a royal flush of photographic evidence. A direct, violent confrontation is out of the question. It would be a messy, emotional affair, and emotion is the enemy of precision. Besides, her death so soon after David's, and with me as the obvious beneficiary of her silence, would paint a target on my back the size of a billboard for Detective Rossi. No, this requires finesse. It requires an accident.

The next morning, I watch her house through my kitchen window, my mind a whirlwind of scenarios. Poison? Unreliable and traceable. A car accident? Too many variables beyond my control. A fall? It worked for James, a tragic echo that appeals to my sense of irony, but the setting must be perfect.

My opportunity reveals itself an hour later, with a timing so perfect it feels like a gift. Sarah emerges, not with her daughter, but with a tall, metal ladder. She struggles to carry it across the lawn and position it against the side of her house, directly beneath a large, second-story window. The window to what I presume is her bedroom or a linen closet. She's going to clean the gutters, or perhaps wash the windows. A mundane, domestic chore. The perfect stage for a tragedy.

My pulse quickens, not with fear, but with the focused anticipation of a surgeon. This is it. The universe is providing the backdrop; I simply need to write the final act.

I move quickly. I find a small, sharp awl in Mark's toolbox, a pointed, inconspicuous tool. I slip it into my pocket. I pull my hair back, put on a pair of thick gardening gloves, and grab a pair of shears from the garage, crafting the image of a neighbor with innocent intentions.

I walk across my lawn, waving brightly. "Sarah! Good morning!"

She looks down from where she's testing the ladder's stability, her face breaking into that warm, genuine smile that now makes my skin crawl. "Chloe! Hi! Just trying to get these gutters cleared before the rain comes."

' Let me help you hold the ladder," I offer, approaching with measured steps. "I'd feel terrible if you fell."

Her face softens with gratitude. "Oh, that's so sweet of you. I hate heights, but someone's got to do it. My husband's away on business this week."

Perfect. No witnesses in the house. No one to interrupt.

She climbs up, rung by rung, and I position myself at the base of the ladder, gripping it with gloved hands, the picture of neighborly assistance. She reaches the top, peering into the gutter, completely focused on her task, completely vulnerable.

This is the moment. One quick movement. A stumble. A tragic fall. The ladder would tip, she would plummet, and I would be the horrified witness who tried to save her. The photograph in her house would be destroyed in the chaos of grief and funeral arrangements before anyone thought to look for it.

I shift my weight, preparing to push.

But then, a voice. Young, high-pitched, calling from inside the house. "Mom? Mom! I can't find my shoes!"

Sarah looks down at me, her expression apologetic. "Sorry, Chloe. Maddie's home sick today. Can you hold on one more second?"

The daughter. Inside. A witness.

My hands freeze on the ladder. The window of opportunity slams shut.

"Of course," I say, my voice steady despite the screaming frustration in my mind. "Take your time."

She descends, hurrying inside to help her daughter, leaving me standing there with the ladder, the awl in my pocket, and a plan that died before it could even begin.

I walk back to my house, my mind already recalculating, reassessing, searching for the next opportunity.

Sarah's death is inevitable. It's just a matter of finding the right moment. And I'm very, very patient.

CHAPTER 18

NOW

The failure with the ladder festers in me for the rest of the day, a corrosive acid of frustration. I had the perfect opportunity and it was snatched away by a simple, domestic detail. I watch their house from my window, the binoculars now a permanent fixture in my hands. I see Maddie playing in the garden, Sarah hanging laundry, the simple, mundane ballet of their lives. Each normal activity feels like a deliberate provocation. They are living in the light, while I am trapped in the shadows they've cast.

Mark emerges from his office around dinner time, his face haggard. The thrumming of his pacing has stopped, replaced by a deep, weary silence. "We need to talk about the money," he says, his voice low and defeated.

My patience, already worn to a thread, snaps. "What about it, Mark? Be precise."

"The fifty thousand. The blackmail," he explains, sinking heavily onto a kitchen stool. "We don't have it, Chloe. The insurance money from David is tied up in probate, and my business account - if I pull a cash amount like that, it'll raise flags with the bank and the tax authorities. We can't fund this without drawing attention."

"We're not paying," I say, my tone leaving no room for argument, crossing my arms.

His eyes widen in genuine terror. "What? We have to! She has a photo of you - "

"Which proves nothing on its own!" I hiss, stepping closer to him, lowering my voice to a sharp edge. "It's a grainy night photo. It could be anyone. It could be doctored. Paying her is an admission of guilt. It makes us slaves to her forever. There will always be another payment, another demand, until we are bled dry. We'd simply be funding her silence, not securing our freedom."

"Then what's your brilliant plan?" he shouts, his composure finally shattering, slapping the granite island with the palm of his hand. "Because so far, your plans have gotten us a detective on our doorstep and a blackmailer living next door! I feel like I'm drowning!"

The air crackles between us. This is the fracture I've been waiting for. The partnership is broken. He is no longer an ally;

he is a witness. A loose end. The thought enters my mind, cold and clear: I will have to deal with him, too. But first, Sarah.

"I have a plan," I say, my voice dropping to a deadly calm, reclaiming control of the space. "But you need to trust me. And you need to follow my lead without question. Can you do that, Mark? Can you put your fear aside long enough to survive?"

He stares at me, and I see the war in his eyes - the remnants of his love for me battling against his primal instinct for self-preservation. The hero complex is dead, replaced by a desperate need for a lifeline. Slowly, he nods, but the trust is gone. It's a nod of desperation, not faith.

"Good," I say. "Then here's what we're going to do." I lean in, and my voice becomes a low, conspiratorial whisper. "We will not pay her. But we will make her believe we are preparing to. We will buy ourselves forty-eight hours of silence, convincing her that the money is coming. Meanwhile, I will gather the leverage I need. I will find a way to break Sarah so utterly that she hands over that photograph and disappears forever. You just need to keep up the appearance of normalcy. Stay home. Be quiet."

I have just bought myself a timeline. The problem of Sarah must be solved within two days, because Mark's inability to hold the line means his usefulness has expired. He is no longer an asset. He is the single greatest threat to my freedom. I need to silence him. Permanently. And I need to do it in a way that points every single ounce of suspicion at our blackmailing neighbor, Sarah. The pieces of a new, more brutal game begin to click into place in my mind.

Two birds. One stone. And forty-eight hours to execute the perfect crime.

CHAPTER 19

THEN

I learned the art of pressure from my father. Not through kindness, but through absence. He was a man who believed emotions were a currency for the weak, and he spent his life hoarding his own, leaving my mother and I in a permanent state of emotional bankruptcy. I watched my mother wither in that vacuum, a beautiful flower starved of sunlight. She would perform ever more elaborate acts of devotion - gourmet meals, a perfectly kept house, meticulously tailored clothes - trying to earn a scrap of his affection, a glimmer of warmth. It never came, and each failure accelerated her decline.

He left us when I was fourteen. No note, no explanation. Just an empty closet and a bank account closed with surgical precision. My mother collapsed inward, becoming a ghost in her own home, barely speaking, fading into the wallpaper.

That's when I understood. Love was a myth. Devotion was a trap designed by the weak. The only real power lay in control. In being the one who applied the pressure, not the one who crumbled under it. I vowed I would never allow myself to be vulnerable to someone else's withdrawal.

I started small. With boys at school. I would identify what they wanted - validation, status, physical affection - and I would dangle it just out of reach, making them perform for it. Their desperation was my reward. It proved my theory correct: human desire was a simple lever, easily manipulated.

James was my first large-scale experiment. He wanted a beautiful, adventurous wife to complete his image of a perfect life, a vibrant accessory. I became that, perfectly. I learned to sail, I laughed a little too loudly at his jokes, I curated a personality that was his ideal. And when I had him utterly convinced, when his identity was fused with mine, I showed him how fragile his perfect world really was. With a sudden gust of wind and a well-placed boom.

His death was not just freedom; it was the ultimate proof of my thesis. I had applied the perfect amount of pressure, and his world had shattered. David was the replication of the experiment, conducted with greater complexity to test my limits. Mark was a variable I introduced specifically to test the limits of external leverage.

But now, with Sarah, the paradigm has shifted. She is not a subject to be manipulated in an experiment. She is a fellow scientist who has entered my lab, attempting to apply pressure to me. She wants to use my past actions as a way to control my present and future. And I have spent a lifetime building an immunity to pressure. She wants to play this game? I will show her what true pressure feels like.

I will not just break her. I will make her beg for the breaking. I will target the central pillar of her emotional life, the one thing she cannot bear to lose, the one vulnerability that guarantees her compliance: her child.

CHAPTER 20

NOW

The plan is elegant in its cruelty. It doesn't require me to lay a hand on Sarah. It requires me to target what she holds most dear, what makes her vulnerable, what she would sacrifice her own freedom to protect.

Two days after the ladder incident, I put the first phase into motion, having monitored her movements with detached professional interest. I wait until I see Sarah and Maddie get into their car and drive away, presumably for school and errands. The house is empty, silent, and unguarded.

I slip out my back door, a small, zippered bag in my hand. I don't go to her house. That would be too risky, too obvious.

I go to the small, wooded park at the end of our street, a place I know Maddie and her friends play after school. I find a secluded spot near the base of a large oak tree, the one with the low, sprawling branch perfect for climbing.

From my bag, I pull out Maddie's favorite hair clip - a blue butterfly one I'd seen her wear repeatedly, which I'd plucked days earlier from their garden fence where it had fallen, treating it as a precious piece of evidence. I press it carefully into the soft earth at the base of the tree, making it look like it was dropped in a struggle or a moment of frantic escape.

Then, I take a small, cheap, pre-paid burner phone from my pocket. It is new, charged, and completely untraceable. I scuff it against the tree bark, then toss it a few feet away, half-hidden under a cluster of ferns, positioned so a small child would stumble upon it immediately. The stage is set. The scene is a perfect picture of a small, sudden struggle.

I return home and wait. My heart is not racing; it is beating a slow, steady rhythm of anticipation. This is the purest form of my art: psychological warfare. The pressure is not applied physically; it is applied through the imagination, exploiting a parent's most fundamental fear.

At 3:30 PM, the school bus rumbles down the street, its mechanical sigh signaling the end of the school day. Maddie gets off, skipping towards her house, her colorful backpack bouncing. Sarah is in the front garden, weeding. I watch from my window, the binoculars pressed to my eyes, a silent, omniscient observer.

Right on schedule, Maddie drops her backpack on the lawn and runs towards the park, drawn by the irresistible promise of the oak tree. "Just for a minute, Mom! I'm going to see if Leo is there!"

"Be back by four, sweetie, before I start dinner!" Sarah calls out, not looking up from her flowers, secure in the knowledge that this street is safe.

I count the seconds. Five minutes. Ten.

Then, I see Maddie running back, her little legs pumping with an urgency that is clearly not play. Her face is pale and distorted with genuine distress. She is crying, great heaving sobs that she can barely contain. She runs straight to her mother, clutching something tightly in her hand.

Sarah looks up, her smile vanishing instantly, replaced by alarm. "Maddie? What's wrong, baby? Did you fall?"

Through her tears, Maddie holds out the burner phone. "I found this! And my clip was on the ground by the big tree! A... a scary man was here before! He ran away into the trees!"

Sarah's face transforms. The calm, friendly mask evaporates entirely, replaced by raw, primal fear. She grabs Maddie, clutching her to her chest with a desperate, crushing intensity, her eyes wide and terrified as she scans the empty park, now seeing not a safe playground, but a hunting ground.

The fear has rooted itself deep.

I lower the binoculars, a slow, cold smile spreading across my face.

Phase one is complete. I have just introduced a predator into her perfect world, exploiting the proximity and the quiet innocence of the neighborhood. I have made her child a target.

The pressure is now entirely on her. Let's see how well she plays defense when the variable is her daughter's safety.

CHAPTER 21

NOW

The effect on Sarah is immediate and profound. The friendly, open woman vanishes, replaced by a skittish, hyper-vigilant sentinel. The next day, I watch as a uniformed security technician installs a new, sophisticated alarm system, cameras mounting under the eaves of her house like mechanical wasps. She no longer lets Maddie play in the front yard unsupervised, her hand a constant, possessive presence on her daughter's shoulder, ushering her directly from the bus to the locked house.

The fear is a living thing, a toxic vapor seeping from their home into mine. It is exactly what I wanted. A frightened person is a predictable person. Their world shrinks, their focus narrows to a single point of survival, and they become blind to the larger threats moving in the periphery - my threat.

Mark, however, is unraveling at an accelerated rate. The sight of the police car that responded to Sarah's frantic call about a "suspicious person" in the park has pushed him closer to the edge. He spends his days locked in his office, but I can hear him pacing, a caged tiger wearing a path in the carpet, mumbling incoherent fears to himself. He jumps at the sound of the doorbell, his head snapping up like a hunted animal, living entirely on nervous adrenaline.

The fifty thousand dollar demand hangs over us, a guillotine blade that I have chosen to ignore, but which dominates his every waking thought.

"She's going to go to the police," he mutters, for what must be the tenth time today. He stands in the doorway of the living room, his frame silhouetted against the hall light, unable to stay in one place for more than a minute. "She has the photo, she has the note, she has the phone. It's all there. It's a chain of evidence."

"The photo is circumstantial," I repeat, my voice calm, though my patience is a thin wire stretched to breaking point. "The note is anonymous. The phone is untraceable. There is no chain. There is only panic, Mark, and panic is what will get us caught."

"I can't live like this," he whispers, and the sound is full of a genuine, breaking despair that cuts through my carefully constructed composure. It is the sound of a man who has reached his limit. "The constant looking over my shoulder, the waiting... I can't do it, Chloe. I haven't slept in three nights. I'm seeing David's face everywhere."

He looks at me, and his eyes are hollow. "I think we should just... talk to someone. A lawyer. Get ahead of this. Tell them David was abusive, tell them I lost control. We can get a lesser sentence."

My blood runs cold. This is the betrayal I have been waiting for. The moment his self-preservation outweighs his loyalty to me, his fantasy of rescue. A lawyer would mean confession. A deal. He would offer me up as the mastermind to save his own skin, painting himself as the manipulated pawn. And they would believe him, because he looks the part of the broken man.

He would sit in a polished office and lay out the entire sordid story, revealing every detail of the plan, every single crack in my perfect narrative. And I would fall with him.

The plan for Sarah must now be accelerated, but Mark has just become a more immediate and dangerous problem. I look at him, this broken, terrified man, and I know with a chilling certainty that his usefulness has expired. He is no longer an asset. He is the single greatest threat to my freedom.

I need to silence him. Permanently. And I need to do it in a way that points every single ounce of suspicion at our blackmailing neighbor, Sarah. The pieces of a new, more brutal game begin to click into place in my mind, forming a clean, efficient solution.

Tomorrow, I will kill Mark. And Sarah will take the fall.

CHAPTER 22

THEN

The first time I realized I could end a life, I was twelve.

It was a squirrel, a mangy, aggressive thing that had been raiding the bird feeder in our backyard, scaring away the beautiful cardinals and blue jays my mother loved to watch. It was a chaotic element, disrupting the small order she clung to.

One afternoon, I found a way to mix a lethal dose of antifreeze with a paste of peanuts and honey. I left the concoction on a small dish near the feeder. The next morning, the squirrel was lying on its side, stiff and cold. Motionless.

My mother was horrified by the sight of the dead creature. My father, however, for the first time I could remember, looked at me with something other than disdain. It was a flicker of assessment. Of recognition. He didn't praise me, but he didn't punish me either. He simply said, "You identified a problem and you found an efficient solution. Wasteful to involve outside help." It was the closest thing to approval I ever received from him.

That lesson became my creed, the bedrock of my operational philosophy: Identify the problem. Find the most efficient solution.

The problem with James was his suffocating vision for our future. The solution was the lake. The problem with David was his oppressive control. The solution was Mark and the fireplace poker. The problem with Mark is his weakness. His inability to hold the line. His sentimental, crumbling conscience. He is a liability who threatens the entire structure. The solution is becoming clear: removal from the board.

And the problem with Sarah is her knowledge. Her evidence. Her arrogant belief that she can control me. Her solution will be more poetic. She sought to apply pressure. She will learn that pressure is a force that can crush as easily as it can contain. She will be the author of her own destruction; I will simply hold the pen.

My father's cold, utilitarian philosophy is the foundation of everything I am. He taught me that sentimentality is a fatal flaw, a vulnerability that invites disaster. That love is a chemical illusion. That the only true constants in life are power and control. He left us because we became a problem he no longer wished to solve. I have simply refined his methodology. I don't abandon my problems. I eliminate them.

CHAPTER 23

NOW

The plan for Mark is simple, brutal, and must look like a tragic accident born of paranoia and guilt. I will use his own fear against him, framing his death as the pathetic surrender of a broken man.

I wait two days, letting the tension in the house thicken to a suffocating syrup. I barely speak to him, offering only monosyllabic answers and pointed silences. I let him stew in his own terror, let the idea of confession take root and grow in the silent, fertile space between us.

Finally, on a night when the wind is howling, mimicking the sound of the storm the night David died, I make my move.

The weather provides the perfect audio camouflage.

I wait until he is in his office, the blue light of his screen illuminating his exhausted face, no doubt staring at the same financial statements that spell out our inability to pay the blackmail. I take a bottle of his favorite Scotch from the cabinet - a rich, single malt he's been saving for a true celebration - and I pour two generous glasses.

Into his, I crush several of the strong sedatives my doctor prescribed for "anxiety" after David's death, grinding them into a fine powder until they are invisible to the naked eye. They dissolve instantly into the amber liquid, their bitterness easily masked by the heavy oak flavor of the whisky.

I carry the glasses to his office and push the door open without knocking, disrupting his quiet misery. He is slumped in his chair, staring out the black window at his own reflection. He flinches violently when I enter, like a child caught stealing.

"I think you're right," I say, my voice soft, conciliatory, the tone of a partner finally giving in to exhaustion. I hold out the spiked glass to him. "We can't go on like this. We need to talk about a new strategy. Something radical."

He looks at the glass, then at me, suspicion warring with his desperate need for a solution, for a partner again. "What kind of strategy? You said we couldn't run."

"A way out," I say, offering a sad, weary smile, meeting his gaze and holding it. "A way to end this. Together. A way to give us both peace."

It's the magic word. Together. He takes the glass. His fingers brush mine, and they are ice cold, clammy with perpetual anxiety.

"I'm sorry," he whispers, his voice cracking. "I'm just... so tired of looking over my shoulder."

"I know," I say, my voice a gentle balm. "Drink. We'll figure this out. We'll find a solution."

He brings the glass to his lips and takes a long, deep swallow, desperate for the false comfort. I watch the muscles in his throat work. I take a small, symbolic sip from my own glass, the clean, untainted whisky burning a path of false camaraderie down my throat.

We talk in circles for twenty minutes. I feed him vague notions of hiring a private investigator to dig up dirt on Sarah, of finding a way to discredit her and frame the note as an elaborate hoax. I feed him hope, and all the while, I watch the sedatives take hold.

His speech begins to slur. His eyelids grow heavy, drooping over his bloodshot eyes. The raw fear in his eyes is slowly replaced by a drugged, placid confusion. He looks peaceful for the first time in weeks.

"I don' feel so good," he slurs, trying to stand from his chair. His legs buckle and he stumbles, catching himself heavily on the desk. "I'm dizzy, Chloe..."

'It's the stress," I say, moving quickly to his side, slipping my shoulder under his arm and guiding his dead weight. "Let's get you to bed. Things will look clearer in the morning. Rest now.'

I half-carry, half-drag his stumbling, heavy form up the stairs, the effort making my back ache. He is mumbling incoherently, a messy jumble of apologies and fears, all dissolving into a thick soup of drugs. I get him into our bedroom and onto the bed. He is out cold within minutes, his breathing deep and stertorous.

This is the moment. The final silence.

The house is still. The storm provides the perfect audio camouflage. I go back downstairs and retrieve the fireplace poker from the stand by the hearth. It's a different one, of course. Lighter. Clean. But the symbolism is everything. It must be the same type of weapon that was used to stage David's death.

I carry it upstairs, my footsteps silent on the plush carpet. I stand over him, looking down at the man who loved me, who killed for me, and who was ready to break for me.

I feel nothing. No anger, no pity, no triumph. Only the quiet, professional focus of a problem-solver. I raise the poker. The wind howls outside, lending a soundtrack of violent justification.

It is not a crime of passion. It is maintenance.

CHAPTER 24

NOW

The sound is wet and final. A sickening crunch that is immediately swallowed by the howl of the wind outside. I stand over Mark, the poker heavy in my hand. His breathing has stopped. The room is preternaturally still, the only sound the frantic drumming of my own heart slowly returning to a normal rhythm. There is surprisingly little blood, a small, dark trickle from his temple against the white pillowcase.

The clinical part of my mind takes over instantly. This is just the first step. The real work begins now, constructing the narrative that will save me.

I wipe the poker clean with a towel from the en suite, erasing my fingerprints, my presence, my sin. I then press his limp fingers around the cool, polished metal, leaving his prints as the sole identity of the user. The weapon of his own destruction, the final, messy act of a broken man.

The staging is everything. The entire weight of the prosecution's belief must be shifted from me to Sarah, and the mechanism for this is Mark's fabricated despair.

I move through the house with a methodical precision. I unlock the back door, leaving it slightly ajar to imply forced entry. I overturn a small table in the hallway, scattering its contents, including a few pieces of his business mail. I find his wallet and remove the cash, stuffing the notes into a kitchen drawer, a clumsy, half-hearted attempt to simulate a robbery - the blackmailer's final act, disrupted by his suicide.

But the masterpiece is in the study.

I sit at his computer, the blue light washing over my determined face. I open his email. My fingers fly across the keyboard, composing a message from his account to my own. The words are frantic, paranoid, perfect.

Chloe, I'm losing my mind. She's watching me. I see her face everywhere. Sarah. She knows. She left another note, under my windscreen wiper. She wants the money tomorrow or she goes to the police. I can't take this. I can't go back to prison. I'd rather be dead. If anything happens to me, it's her. I did this for you.

I send the email. The digital timestamp is my alibi, documenting his final, frantic state of mind.

I then open a new browser window. I search for local news articles about the break-in at David's apartment, about his death. I search for "blackmail laws UK" and "punishment for accessory to murder." I leave the tabs open, a digital portrait of a mind spiraling into obsession, fear, and a sense of deep, final guilt.

Finally, I take the burner phone I used in the park to terrify Sarah. I wipe it down meticulously and press it into the pocket of his jacket, hanging in the hall closet, near the staged robbery. The final piece of the puzzle. The undeniable, physical connection between his paranoia and the woman next door.

I survey my work.

The scene tells a clear, tragic story: Mark, consumed by guilt and terror over David's death, is being blackmailed by our neighbor, Sarah. Driven to the brink, he takes his own life, staging a break-in to muddy the waters and pointing the finger at his tormentor in his suicide note.

It is elegant. It is efficient.

I walk to the bathroom and look at myself in the mirror. My face is pale, but my eyes are clear and unnervingly calm. There is no hysteria. No regret. Only the quiet, professional satisfaction of a problem solved.

I take a deep breath, filling my lungs with the stale, heavy air.

Then I scream.

It is a raw, piercing sound of pure, manufactured terror, a sound designed to shatter the quiet of the night and bring the world running. The performance is about to begin.

CHAPTER 25
NOW

The police arrive in a whirlwind of blue lights and crackling radios, slicing through the suburban silence. The driveway is instantly choked with official vehicles, casting garish red and blue shadows across the manicured lawn.

I am the picture of devastation. Huddled on the bottom step of the staircase, wrapped in a blanket an officer placed over my shoulders, I tremble with a violence that is only partly feigned. The adrenaline is a live wire in my veins, but the control remains absolute.

I tell my story in broken fragments, just as I rehearsed. "I was in the bath... I heard a noise... a crash... I came out and the back door was open... I called for Mark... I found him..." I punctuate the sentences with dry, racking sobs, ensuring my distress is palpable but not hysterical enough to impede the process.

Detective Rossi is there within twenty minutes, her sharp eyes missing nothing, scanning the staged chaos of the hallway before landing on me. She doesn't offer comfort. She simply observes, a hawk circling wounded prey, her clipboard held tight.

"Mrs. Sterling," she says, her voice neutral, professional. "Can you walk me through it again, slowly?"

I do. I pour every ounce of my performance into it, letting tears I've conjured from a well of sheer will streak down my face. I tell her about Mark's recent paranoia, his sleepless nights, his fear that "someone was watching him." I make sure the details are precise enough to sound credible, vague enough to avoid direct lies.

I do not mention Sarah. Not directly. The seed has been planted in the email. It must be them who finds it, not me who points the finger.

As if on cue, an officer emerges from the study, his face grim. "Detective? You'll want to see this. He left something on his computer."

Rossi gives me a final, inscrutable look before following him. I watch her go, my heart hammering against my ribs, but with anticipation, not fear. This is the moment. She is reading the email. She is seeing the search history. She is constructing the narrative I built for her.

She returns ten minutes later, her expression grim, but now tinged with a new, professional focus. "It appears your husband was under significant duress, Mrs. Sterling. We found an email he sent you, and his computer history... he was being blackmailed."

I look up, widening my eyes in a perfect blend of shock and dawning horror. "Blackmailed? By who? Who would do such a terrible thing?"

Rossi's gaze is like a laser, dissecting my reaction. "He mentions a name. Sarah. Your neighbor."

The sound I make is a choked gasp, a masterpiece of revelation and betrayal. "No... It can't be. She's been so kind. She brought me food... She talked about her daughter..." I let the sentence hang, painting the picture of a woman utterly betrayed by the kindness of strangers.

"We'll need to speak with her," Rossi says, her tone leaving no room for argument. She turns to another officer. "Bring Mrs. Jenkins in for questioning. Now."

As they move to execute her order, Rossi turns back to me, lowering her voice. "We'll need a formal statement from you at the station. And we'll need to take your husband's computer, his phone, and the weapon."

"Of course," I whisper, pulling the blanket tighter, shrinking into the victim role. "Anything to help. I just want this nightmare to end."

I watch them leave, the emergency vehicles slowly dispersing. Through the window, I can see lights flickering on in Sarah's house, can see the shadows of officers at her door. The trap is springing shut.

I lean back against the staircase, allowing myself the smallest, most private smile.

Everything is going exactly according to plan.

CHAPTER 26

THEN

There is a particular silence that follows a perfectly executed plan. It's not an empty silence. It's a full, resonant quiet, humming with the satisfaction of a problem solved and all variables accounted for. I felt it after James was pulled from the lake, the concerned murmurs of the coroner a soothing background noise to my inner peace. I felt it after David, standing on my sister's doorstep, the weight of his death a comfortable cloak around my shoulders.

And I feel it now, sitting in my sterile living room after the police have taken Mark's body away. The chaos is gone. The variable of his weakness has been eliminated. The physical and emotional noise he generated has been surgically removed, leaving a profound vacuum. This is my natural state. This calm. This control.

The world believes that grief is loud, a messy, public spectacle of tears and anguish. They don't understand that true, profound loss - or in my case, a perfect victory - is a quiet thing. It is the silence of a chessboard after checkmate. The game is over. The opponent is gone. All that remains is the analysis, the quiet review of the moves that led to victory.

I look around my beautiful, empty house. It is mine again. Truly mine. The last vestige of a shared life has been scrubbed away. The air is clean, devoid of the stale adrenaline and fear Mark had infused it with.

Soon, the police will finish with Sarah. They will find the binoculars. They will match the font on her printer to the blackmail note. They will find the pressure I apply will be irresistible. She will break. She will confess to the blackmail. And with Mark's "suicide note" implicating her, the circle will be complete. David's case will be quietly reclassified. A tragic story of a man driven to murder by a blackmailer, who then took his own life.

Two birds, one stone. An efficient solution.

The silence is beautiful. It is the sound of my freedom. I sit for a long time, allowing the profound quiet to settle deep in my bones, relishing the absolute, hard-won control. This is the reward.

CHAPTER 27

NOW

They question Sarah for six hours. I watch from my window as she is led from her house, her face a mask of stunned confusion. Maddie is left with a female officer, a small, terrified figure on the porch, clinging to the uniformed leg. I feel a flicker of something - not guilt, but a cold recognition of the collateral damage. The child is an unfortunate necessity. A piece in her mother's game, just as Mark was in mine.

Detective Rossi returns to my house late in the afternoon. Her face is unreadable, but I sense a new tension in her posture. A simmering frustration. She sits opposite me in the living room, the weight of her scrutiny heavier than before.

"Mrs. Jenkins is maintaining her innocence," she says, watching me carefully for a reaction. "She admits to owning binoculars but claims she's a birdwatcher. She denies any knowledge of the blackmail or sending any notes."

I allow a look of pained confusion to cross my face, a perfect blend of shock and doubt. "But... the email... Mark was so sure. He was in such distress."

"The email is compelling," Rossi concedes, rubbing her temple as if the narrative is giving her a headache. "But it's not concrete proof. And we found no evidence on her computer or her phone. No drafts of the note, no record of the photograph. She's either meticulous, or she's telling the truth about the blackmail."

My blood runs cold. She's smarter than I gave her credit for. She's covering her tracks, or she truly is innocent of the notes.

"There is, however, another complication," Rossi continues, her eyes locking with mine, forcing me to hold her gaze. "The autopsy on Mr. Sterling will take time, but the initial assessment of the head wound is... curious."

"Curious?" I echo, my voice barely a whisper, forcing myself to project confusion, though my mind is screaming for certainty.

"The angle of the blow," she says, her words deliberate, slow, and precise. "It's not consistent with a self-inflicted injury. The force required and the trajectory suggest the strike came from someone else. Someone standing over him."

The room tilts violently. I grip the edge of the sofa to steady myself. This is a variable I did not anticipate. I was too focused on the narrative, not the forensic science. I replayed the moment a hundred times in my head: me, standing over his drugged body, the poker raised. Of course, the angle was wrong. It was a blind spot, a stupid, amateur mistake born of rushing.

"I don't understand," I stammer, the fear in my voice now entirely genuine, impossible to fake. "You're saying... someone was in our house? Someone killed him, and it wasn't a suicide?"

"It's a possibility we are exploring," Rossi says, her gaze unwavering, seeing the first, true crack in my performance. "Which is why, Mrs. Sterling, I need you to think very carefully. Is there anything else you remember? Any detail, no matter how small, that might help us understand what happened here?"

I shake my head, my mind racing through the variables, the options, the exits. The perfect plan is unraveling. The angle of the blow. A single, forensic detail threatening to undo everything.

"I've told you everything I know," I whisper. "I just want this nightmare to end."

Rossi stands, her eyes never leaving mine. "We'll be in touch. Don't leave town, Mrs. Sterling. We have more questions."

As she walks out, I sit frozen on the sofa, my carefully constructed world crumbling around me. For the first time in my life, I don't have the next move planned.

For the first time, I might actually lose.

CHAPTER 28

NOW

The silence in the house after Rossi leaves is deafening. It is no longer the quiet of victory, but the heavy, waiting silence of a tomb.

The forensic evidence has shifted everything. My careful staging of Mark's suicide is now a liability - the angle of the blow that seemed perfect in the moment has become the smoking gun. I was too focused on the narrative, on controlling Sarah and the blackmail story, to consider the cold mathematics of trajectory and force. A rookie mistake dressed up as brilliance.

I pace the living room, my mind racing, scrambling for a new foothold. Sarah is still the key. She must be. The entire structure of my defense rests on her being the villain. If she is innocent, then the blackmail narrative collapses. And if the blackmail narrative collapses, then Mark's "suicide" becomes a murder. And I become the only logical suspect.

The problem is clear: I need to break her. I need her to confess, not just to blackmail, but to escalating the pressure to the point of murder. But she is protected now. The police have her. Her house is a crime scene. I can't get to her directly.

There is another way.

I stop pacing. My eyes drift across the street, to Sarah's house The lights are on. Maddie is home, likely with a family member or a social worker. A frightened, vulnerable little girl.

A new, terrible plan begins to form. It is the most ruthless one yet. The last barrier of morality I had retained, the one that kept me from striking the ladder in front of the child, dissolves completely. If I cannot make Sarah confess to save herself, perhaps I can make her confess to save her daughter.

I will use the panic I have already seeded, twisting the narrative of the predator in the park into something far more personal, far more immediate. I will make Sarah believe her daughter is in mortal danger. And I will make her believe that only a confession - a public, recorded confession - will save Maddie's life.

It is monstrous. It is necessary. And it is my only way out.

CHAPTER 29

THEN

I learned about leverage from my mother.

After my father left, she was a ghost. She moved through the house as if her feet didn't touch the floor, her eyes vacant, lost in a grief that was less about a husband's departure and more about the collapse of her entire worldview. She stopped cooking, stopped cleaning. The world lost its color. I was fifteen, and the hunger was a constant, gnawing presence in my belly. The cupboards were bare. The electricity was due to be shut off - a cold, bureaucratic threat that terrified her more than any emotional confrontation.

I found her jewelry box - the last thing of value we owned, representing the small, fragile security of our past. It held a string of pearls from her mother and my father's old college ring, heavy and gold. I took them to a pawn shop in a part of town where they didn't ask questions. The man behind the counter offered me a fraction of their worth, his gaze cynical and disinterested. I didn't argue. I took the cash and I bought groceries. I paid the electric bill.

When my mother realized the box was gone, she didn't cry. She just looked at me, and for a single, fleeting moment, there was a spark of something in her dead eyes. It wasn't gratitude. It was recognition. Acknowledgment that I had done what was necessary, brutal as it was. That I had applied the leverage required - sacrificing her sentimentality for our basic survival - to make our life continue. It was the last meaningful interaction we ever had. She checked out for good after that, her spirit broken by the transaction.

But she had taught me the final, crucial lesson. True power isn't just about eliminating problems. It's about understanding what people value most and being willing to hold it hostage. For David, it was his reputation and control. For Mark, it was his freedom and his need for salvation.

For Sarah, that is Maddie. Her child is the absolute, immovable center of her existence, and therefore, her greatest weakness. It is the lock I can't break, but the lever I can use. This realization, dark as it was, settled the final argument in my mind the trap for Sarah needed to be absolute, and nothing is more absolute than a mother's terror.

CHAPTER 30

NOW

The night is my ally. It always has been. It is a canvas of shadows and muffled sounds, perfect for the deployment of terror.

I wait until the last police cruiser leaves Sarah's house, a deliberate action to avoid direct contact with law enforcement. The house is quiet, but the light remains on upstairs - Maddie's room. Her grandmother, the last line of defense, arrived an hour ago, a frail-looking woman with a pinched, worried face. She is the perfect conduit for maximum impact.

I am a shadow in my own garden. I have the second burner phone, the one I kept in reserve, a necessary security protocol against the eventual collapse of the first one. My fingers are steady as I type a new message. Not to Sarah; she won't have her phone. This one is to the landline number I memorized from the grandmother's frantic call to the police earlier, a number easily found in the online directory. The method is untraceable and bypasses the current police lock on the house.

The message is not long. It is not detailed. It is a surgical strike aimed directly at the grandmother's primal fear, designed to generate maximum terror and immediate action, leveraging the fear I planted days ago with the hair clip and the first burner phone

Confess to the blackmail. Tell them you drove Mark Sterling to suicide. If you don't, the man in the park won't just drop a phone next time. He will take your daughter. You have until noon tomorrow.

I do not send it from my location. I drive five miles away, to a quiet retail park near the motorway exit, and send it from there, ensuring the cell tower ping is nowhere near my home. Then I dispose of the phone, dropping it deep into a storm drain where it will be irretrievable. The action is clean. Untraceable.

I return home and go to bed. I sleep deeply, dreamlessly. The satisfaction of having executed the most brutal, final move of the game ensures my rest.

The next morning, I am woken by the sound of a car door slamming. I go to the window. Detective Rossi is walking up Sarah's path, her stride purposeful. She is clearly responding to the threat, the pressure immediately relayed by the grandmother.

I watch, my breath held, as the door opens. I cannot hear the words, but I see the grandmother's hand fly to her mouth in shock. I see her nod, frantically, and point inside, indicating the urgent message she received. Rossi disappears into the house.

Thirty minutes later, my doorbell rings. Rossi stands on my porch, her expression grim, but now bearing the look of a detective who has found her necessary conclusion. "Mrs. Sterling. We've had a development. Sarah Jenkins has confessed to the blackmail."

A wave of pure, unadulterated triumph washes over me, but I conceal it behind a hand pressed to my mouth, simulating shock. "My God," I whisper. "Why? Why would she suddenly do that?"

"She claims she was in financial trouble. She saw an opportunity after your husband's death," Rossi says, her voice flat, recounting the false motive. "She admitted to taking the photograph and sending the notes. The pressure, she says, drove your husband to... his decision."

It is done. The narrative is sealed. I am safe. Sarah has chosen the certainty of a blackmail conviction over the terror of her daughter's disappearance.

I allow a single, perfect tear to trace a path down my cheek. It is a tear of victory. "I... I don't know what to say. It's too much."

"There's nothing to say," Rossi replies, her voice flat, the official closure grating against her instinct. "It's over. The case is moving to the Crown Prosecution Service."

But as she turns to leave, she pauses. She looks back at me, and her dark eyes hold mine for a beat too long, seeing past the tears and the performance. "It's a tidy ending, isn't it?" she says. "Almost too tidy."

Then she walks away, leaving me standing in the doorway, the chill of her doubt settling deep in my bones. The game is not over. It has simply found a new, more determined player in Detective Rossi.

CHAPTER 31

NOW

The days that follow are a study in quiet tension. The official narrative is set in stone: Sarah Jenkins, a desperate woman, blackmailed a grieving man, driving him to suicide. The case is closed, at least in the eyes of the public and the majority of the precinct.

But Detective Rossi's final words are a splinter in my mind, festering. "Almost too tidy." She doesn't visit again, but I feel her presence like a constant, low-grade hum, an electrical current running beneath the surface of my new life. I see an unmarked car parked down the street for two days straight before it moves on. They are watching me. They are waiting for me to make a mistake.

I am a ghost in my own home. I move from room to room, the silence now feeling accusatory. The triumph I felt has curdled into a sharp, focused paranoia. Rossi is not like the others. She is not fooled by performances; she is immune to the victim narrative. She operates on instinct, a bloodhound that has caught a scent it refuses to abandon, and that scent is me.

The problem is no longer Sarah. The problem is Rossi. She is the single, persistent variable that threatens the structural integrity of my acquired freedom.

And the solution is not clear. I cannot eliminate a detective; that is a game with stakes too high, a board too large, involving an entire justice system I cannot hope to defeat directly. My power lies in the intimate, the domestic, the psychological. Not in a war with the state.

I need to understand my enemy. I need to find her pressure point, her vulnerability, the one thing she cares about more than closing the Mark Sterling case.

I sit at my laptop, the screen reflecting my grim determination. The only way to stop a hunter is to give her a bigger, shinier quarry to chase. I need to know what drives Maria Rossi, what unfinished business haunts her. I will weaponize her professional obsession.

CHAPTER 32

THEN

Perfection is an illusion. It is a destination that does not exist.

I learned this not from a failure, but from my greatest success. The death of James was perfect. Flawless in its execution and its aftermath. And yet, it left me empty. The high faded almost instantly. The boredom returned, corrosive and profound.

That was the lesson. The goal is not the perfection of a single act. It is the mastery of the game itself. The ability to adapt, to improvise, to turn your opponent's strengths against them. Perfection is static; mastery is fluid.

David was a different kind of challenge. He was more observant than James, more controlling. The plan had to be more complex, involving another player, Mark, to introduce an element of believable chaos. It was messier. It had more variables. And because of that, the satisfaction was deeper, more sustained.

Mark's elimination was messier still. It required a rushed staging and has now attracted the attention of a tenacious detective who sees through my core narrative. Each problem has been more complex than the last. Each solution has been more difficult to engineer. And with each victory, the stakes are raised.

Rossi is the most complex problem I have ever faced. She is intelligent, intuitive, and her authority is her armor. She seeks truth, a concept I have spent my life manipulating. To win this game, I will need to do more than just eliminate a problem. I will need to break her will. I will need to make her doubt not just the evidence, but her own instincts. I will need to provide her with a conclusion so compelling, so seemingly genuine, that she turns her relentless gaze to the past.

I will need to become a ghost she can never catch because she will be too busy chasing the ghosts I provide for her.

CHAPTER 33

NOW

I begin my research on Detective Maria Rossi. It is a delicate operation, conducted from the shadows, using layers of encryption and disposable search accounts. I use public records, local news articles, the faint digital footprint of a careful, professional person.

The data is sparse, but telling. She is divorced. No children. Lives alone with a dog - a predictable profile for a career obsessed with solving other people's problems. Her work is her life. She has a commendation for closing a difficult cold case, but then I find the counterpoint: a murder that was never solved, a trail that went cold - the murder of a young woman five years ago. The file was never officially closed, the media had moved on, but the article implies it was a personal failure for her, a case that haunts her professional reputation and her conscience.

A cold case. A personal failure. A vulnerability.

An idea begins to glimmer in the dark recesses of my mind. A terrible, audacious idea that requires a level of fabrication and risk I've never attempted.

What if I could give her a new solution to her old failure? What if I could offer her a killer, neatly tied up and conveniently deceased? Not the real killer, of course, but a plausible one. A patsy. A name from the past that I could carefully, artfully, connect to that old, dead case.

I would be giving her a gift. The closure she desperately wants, the vindication she needs to rebuild her professional self-esteem. I would be validating her instincts, proving her right, and in doing so, I would redirect her relentless gaze away from me and onto a phantom she couldn't resist chasing.

It is a high-risk strategy. It involves digging into a world I know nothing about. But the beauty of it is its simplicity: I am not fighting her. I am helping her. I am using her own obsession as the tool of my salvation.

I lean back from my computer, a slow, cold smile spreading across my face. I have found Rossi's pressure point. Her need for justice. And I am going to use it to bury her.

CHAPTER 34

NOW

The plan to manipulate Detective Rossi is a high-wire act over an abyss, requiring a precision that makes my previous schemes look like child's play. It demands more than just planting evidence; it requires weaving a ghost, crafting a narrative so compelling it will override her suspicion of me and consume her professional obsessions.

I spend the next forty-eight hours in a state of focused mania, my world shrinking to the glow of my laptop screen and the scattered notes that now paper the walls of my spare room. This is my war room, and the battle is for my future.

The first step is to understand the victim in Rossi's cold case. Her name was Anna Clarke. Twenty-four years old, a junior graphic designer, found strangled in a public park five years ago. The case went nowhere. No witnesses, no DNA, no obvious motive. The media dubbed it the "Park Angel" killing, a name that makes my skin crawl with its sentimentality. The police concluded it was random, an attack by a stranger.

A random attack is useless to me. I need a connection. A thread I can pull.

I delve deeper, into the digital archives of local newspapers, social media groups Anna belonged to, anything to build a profile. I learn she was quiet, a lover of books and old films. She had a small, tight-knit group of friends. And then I find it, buried in a friend's nostalgic social media post from two years ago, a photograph of Anna at a birthday party.

She is laughing, holding a cocktail, and standing next to her, with his arm slung casually around her shoulder, is a man I never expected to see: James. My James.

The air leaves my lungs in a sudden rush. The world seems to tilt on its axis. I stare at the screen, my mind reeling, trying to process this impossible connection. James and Anna Clarke. They knew each other. How? Why did he never mention her? The photo is from a year before his death, before I had even met him. This changes everything. It's a thread, yes, but it's a thread that leads directly back to me, a thread I cannot afford for Rossi to find independently.

A cold sweat breaks out on the back of my neck. This is too close. Far too close. I consider abandoning this entire line of attack, but the sheer, terrifying coincidence feels like a sign. A challenge. Or a trap.

I study the photo more closely. James is smiling, but it doesn't reach his eyes. It's the same polished, public smile he used with clients. Anna is looking up at him with an expression of open admiration. Was it an affair? A flirtation that turned sour? James was a charismatic man, the kind who drew people in. The kind who could make a young woman feel special before sailing away on a lake and leaving her behind.

A new, more audacious idea begins to form, born from this unexpected connection. What if I don't need to invent a killer? What if the killer was already there, all along? What if James killed Anna Clarke?

The thought is electrifying. It makes a dark, twisted sense. The timeline fits. The lack of a clear motive fits the profile of a man who saw people as possessions, who could discard them when they became inconvenient. Had Anna threatened to tell his wife? Had she demanded more than he was willing to give? It was exactly the kind of problem he would have sought to eliminate. He was a man who believed in efficient solutions, just like his father. Just like me.

This is the key. I won't be fabricating a story from whole cloth; I will be revealing a hidden truth. A truth that died with James on that lake. I can craft the evidence to point to him. A forgotten trophy, a cryptic note in his handwriting that I can forge, an anonymous tip suggesting he was seen arguing with Anna around the time of her death. I can tie up Rossi's cold case with a neat, tragic bow, and in doing so, I will make my own history with James a layer of insulation. I will be the poor widow who unknowingly married a killer, a victim twice over.

The sheer, brutal elegance of it takes my breath away. I am no longer just covering up my own crimes. I am solving another. I will give Detective Rossi the closure she craves, I will validate her instincts, and I will permanently shift her gaze from a living, breathing threat to a dead, convenient one.

I look at the photograph of James and Anna one last time before closing the tab. A strange, cold feeling settles in my stomach. It isn't guilt. It's something closer to kinship. We both loved the same man, in our own ways. And we were both, ultimately, his problems. The difference is, I was the one who solved him.

Now, I will use his memory to solve my final, most dangerous problem. I pick up a pen and begin to sketch out the blueprint of my masterpiece. It will require every ounce of my skill, every shred of my nerve. But for the first time since Rossi looked at me with those knowing eyes, I feel a flicker of something I thought I had lost. Hope.

CHAPTER 35

NOW

The plan is a house of cards, beautiful in its complexity and terrifying in its fragility. A single misplaced breath could bring it all down. I spend the next week in a state of hyper-focused obsession, my every waking moment dedicated to the meticulous construction of my lie. My world shrinks to the glow of my laptop screen and the scattered notes that now paper the walls of my spare room, maps of old neighborhoods and articles about cold cases. This is my war room, and the battle is for my future.

The first step is the evidence itself. It must be compelling enough to reopen a cold case, yet vague enough to be untraceable back to me. The objective is plausible suspicion, not airtight conviction - Rossi will handle the conviction once her professional pride is engaged.

I start with the "trophy." Anna Clarke was reported to be wearing a silver locket when she disappeared, a piece that was never found. I spend two days scouring online antique markets until I find a passable replica, a tarnished, heart-shaped thing that looks old enough to be believable. I don't need it to be the real locket; I just need it to be plausible. I carefully tuck a tiny, faded photograph of a generic flower inside - the kind that might have come with the frame - and seal it shut. The detail is crucial; it suggests sentimental value. The next day, I take a long drive to a park on the other side of the city, one with a similar topography to where Anna's body was found, choosing an area I've never visited before. Under the cover of a moonless night, I bury the locket shallowly near the roots of a large, distinctive oak tree, a location I will later "anonymously" reveal. It is placed just deep enough to require effort to find, adding to its archaeological credibility.

The second piece is the note. I still have a few of James's old business planners in a box of his things I'd never gotten around to discarding - a testament to the dangers of sentimentality. I find a page with minimal writing and practice for hours, tracing the loops and slants of his handwriting until I can replicate it with chilling accuracy. I write a single, cryptic line on a torn piece of paper from the same planner: "A.C. - too demanding. Becoming a problem. Must end it. -J" I age the paper with a careful application of coffee grounds and a few minutes in a low oven, simulating years of neglect. I then seal it in a plastic bag. This, I will plant in a different, even more indirect way.

The final piece is the most dangerous: the anonymous tip. I need to lead Rossi to the evidence without her suspecting the hand that guides her. I spend days researching the cold case online forums, identifying the most dedicated, slightly unhinged amateur sleuths - the people Rossi would naturally ignore but would inevitably monitor. I create a new, untraceable email account and craft a message to one of them, a man who posts long, conspiracy-laced theories about the case. My message is a masterclass in suggestion, posing as a "guilty conscience" who knew James Sterling years ago, mentioning his "volatile temper" and his "secret affair" with a young woman he only refers to as "A." I don't mention the locket or the note. I simply plant the seed of James's name and his connection to Anna. I know this man will take this "lead" and run with it, broadcasting it to the forum, where I am certain Rossi or one of her colleagues still monitors.

The work is exhausting. It requires a level of sustained concentration I haven't needed since the days leading up to David's murder. I sleep fitfully, my dreams filled with shifting faces - James, David, Mark, Anna, Rossi - all merging into one accusing mask. I am constantly looking over my shoulder, paranoid that Rossi is watching my every move, that she can see the ghost I am building right in front of her. The psychological toll of living entirely within a fabrication is immense.

A week after I send the email, I allow myself to check the forum. My heart hammers against my ribs as I scroll. And there it is. A new, lengthy post from the amateur sleuth, his digital excitement palpable. The subject line reads: "BREAKTHROUGH? New Lead Points to James Sterling in 'Park Angel' Case!" The post details the "tip" he received, speculating wildly about James's business dealings and his "mysterious" death.

The seed has been planted. Now, I must wait for the detective to take the bait.

The waiting is its own special kind of torture. Every ring of the doorbell, every phone call, sends a jolt of adrenaline through me. I am a spider sitting at the edge of a web I have woven, feeling for the slightest vibration. I have done all I can. The evidence is planted, the rumor is sown. The rest is out of my hands. All I can do is maintain my performance as the grieving, twice-widowed wife, a woman so steeped in tragedy that she could never be the architect of it.

I pour a glass of wine and stand by the window, looking out at the quiet street. The silence feels different now. It is no longer empty, but charged, pregnant with the impending collision of my carefully constructed past and Rossi's relentless pursuit of the truth. A truth I have meticulously crafted just for her.

CHAPTER 36

NOW

The waiting is a slow, corrosive acid. Each day that passes without a word from Detective Rossi feels like a reprieve and a sentence all at once. Has she seen the forum post? Has she taken the bait, allowing her professional ambition to override her instinct? Or has she dismissed it as the ramblings of an internet conspiracy theorist, her focus remaining laser-sharp on me?

I find myself trapped in a prison of my own making. The house, once a symbol of my victory, now feels like a gilded cage with glass walls. Every creak of the floorboards is a footstep. Every ring of the phone is her voice on the other end, finally delivering the accusation I know is coming. My performance for the outside world must be flawless, but inside, the walls are closing in.

I try to maintain a routine to ward off the paranoia. I am in the grocery store every Tuesday morning. I take my walk at precisely 3 p.m. I am in bed by 10:30. I am the most uninteresting woman in England, every action a carefully choreographed ballet of banality.

I feel Rossi's frustration like a physical force. She wants me to break, to run, to do something - anything that will confirm her suspicions. I give her nothing but the steady, placid surface of a life recovering from trauma.

And then, the first crack appears. Not in my facade, but in hers.

I am returning from my afternoon walk when a car pulls up beside me. It's not an unmarked sedan; it's Rossi's personal car, a modest, slightly worn hatchback. The window rolls down slowly, revealing her tired, drawn face, dark circles under her eyes testifying to her lack of rest.

"Mrs. Sterling," she says, her voice lacking its usual professional crispness. "A moment?"

"Of course, Detective," I say, my voice gentle with feigned concern, stopping precisely three feet from the car door. "Is everything alright? You look exhausted."

She doesn't answer directly. "The name James Sterling has come up in connection with an old case of mine. Anna Clarke."

I allow a look of polite confusion to cross my face, carefully curated to show no flicker of recognition or fear, only the mild curiosity of a stranger. "James? My James? But... how? It's been years since his accident."

"That's what I'm trying to determine," she says, her eyes searching mine for a tell, a twitch, anything. "Did he ever mention a woman named Anna Clarke?"

I furrow my brow, looking down at the pavement as if searching my memory for a phantom name. "Anna Clarke... no, I don't believe so. It's not a familiar name. He had so many business associates, though. It's possible." I pause, then look back at her, my expression open and helpful. "What is this about, Detective? Is this connected to the David case somehow?"

She hesitates, and in that hesitation, I see it: the seed has taken root. My anonymous tip has worked its way into the official investigation. She is no longer just looking at me; she is looking through me, into the past, at the ghost of my dead husband.

"It's probably nothing," she says finally, the dismissal hollow. "Just tying up loose ends on a very old file. Thank you for your time."

She drives away, and I continue my walk home, my steps measured and calm. But inside, a fierce, silent celebration is underway. She took the bait. The narrative is shifting. The hunter is now following a different scent, one I laid for her. The pressure on me is easing, its weight transferred to the shoulders of a dead man. Patience is not just a virtue. It is a weapon. And I have just fired my most precise shot yet.

I later verify my suspicion. I am returning from my next walk, approaching the street, when I see a flicker of movement in an upstairs window of Sarah's now-empty house. A brief glint of light, like the sun reflecting off a lens. My blood runs cold - Rossi isn't just waiting; she's watching. She has someone stationed in the house across the street, using it as a perfect vantage point to observe my every move. The unmarked car was just the obvious play; this is the real surveillance.

A cold fury mixes with the fear. She is treating me like a subject, a bug under a microscope. She is studying my patterns, waiting for me to slip. I don't break my stride. I don't look up. I keep walking, my face a mask of tranquil contemplation, but my mind is racing. This changes the calculus of my plan entirely. Any move I make, any deviation from my carefully constructed persona, will be noted. Planting the forged note from James, the next step in my scheme, is now impossibly risky. Under the gaze of a police surveillance team, every action is magnified, every motive questioned.

I return home, the familiar walls now feeling transparent. I feel exposed, naked. I pour a drink, my hand trembling slightly. The game has entered a new, more dangerous phase. Rossi is no longer just an investigator; she is a hunter, and I am the prey in her sights. My plan to frame James is brilliant, but it is static. It requires action, and right now, any action is perilous.

I need a new approach. A passive one. I need the evidence to find its way to Rossi without my direct involvement. I need to become a spectator in my own defense, to let the narrative I've set in motion unfold on its own. But passivity is a foreign language to me. My entire life has been defined by decisive, calculated action. I stand in the center of my living room, the silence of the house pressing in on me. For the first time, I feel a flicker of genuine doubt. Have I finally met my match? The glint in the window across the street was a message. A reminder. The hunt is on.

CHAPTER 37

NOW

The air itself feels different after Rossi's visit. The constant, oppressive weight of being watched begins to lessen. Within days, the glint from the window across the street vanishes. The unmarked car does not return. My strategy of passive resistance has worked; I have bored them into redirecting their resources. The investigation is now officially elsewhere, chasing the ghost of James Sterling.

A part of me wants to revel in this victory, to pour a glass of expensive wine and toast my own genius. But the professional in me knows this is the most dangerous time. Complacency is the precursor to failure. Rossi is not a woman who gives up easily. She has simply shifted her focus, and I must be ready for the moment she circles back.

I allow myself one small, calculated deviation from my routine. I drive to a library three towns over, a place with no connection to me or my life. Here, using their public computers, I delve back into the online forum.

The thread about James and the "Park Angel" case has exploded. The amateur sleuths are having a field day, connecting dots that don't exist, building a compelling fiction upon the foundation I provided. They have dug up old photos of James, analyzed his business dealings for "shady connections," and one user even claims to have seen him arguing with a woman matching Anna's description - a pure fabrication that the others have eagerly accepted as fact.

It is working better than I could have hoped. The hive mind is doing my work for me, creating a cloud of plausible suspicion around James's name. This is the passive approach I needed. The noise they are generating gives Rossi more than enough reason to officially re-examine James in relation to the cold case, justifying her shift in focus to her superiors.

I log off, wiping my history, a ghost in the machine once more. As I drive home, the grey sky begins to release a soft, persistent rain. It feels like a cleansing, washing away the last traces of my direct involvement. The plan is in the wild now, a living thing growing on its own. My role is done.

But as I turn onto my street, a different kind of chill settles over me. Parked in my driveway is a car I recognize. It's not a police car. It's the sleek, black sedan belonging to David's brother, Robert.

I haven't seen him since the funeral. He never liked me. David was the successful one, the one who escaped their modest upbringing, and Robert always viewed me as the glamorous accessory who completed that picture. He saw me as a gold-digger, though he never dared say it to David's face.

What is he doing here?

I pull in behind him, my mind racing through possibilities. He couldn't know anything. He has no connection to any of this. This must be about the estate, the life insurance money that is finally being released. Yes, that must be it. A simple, unpleasant matter of business.

I put on my pleasant, weary widow's face and step out of the car into the rain. He gets out of his, a tall, dour man in an ill-fitting suit, holding a manila envelope.

"Chloe," he says, his voice as grim as his expression. No condolences, no pleasantries.

"Robert. This is a surprise. Is everything alright?"

"No," he says bluntly, his eyes hard. "I don't think it is." He holds out the envelope, its edges softened by moisture. "I think you and I need to talk."

CHAPTER 38

NOW

I lead Robert into the living room, my heart a frantic bird against my ribs. The carefully restored peace of my home is shattered by his antagonistic presence. He sits on the edge of an armchair, back rigid, radiating quiet accusation, while I take the sofa, arranging myself to look vulnerable yet composed.

"What's this about, Robert?" I ask, gesturing to the manila envelope he's placed on the coffee table between us, making the gesture seem weary.

"It's about David," he says, his gaze unwavering, a heavy, judgmental weight. "And Mark. And you."

The directness of his accusation is a physical blow. I keep my face a mask of confused concern. "I don't understand. Why would you include Mark in this?"

"David's death never sat right with me," he says, his voice low and steady, fueled by righteous anger. "A break-in? In that neighborhood? It felt... staged. And then Mark, your lover, kills himself out of guilt days after the police question you? It's a very neat story, Chloe. Too neat."

"Robert, that's a horrible thing to say," I whisper, letting my voice tremble, deploying a perfect look of hurt. "We've been through so much..."

"Have you?" he interrupts, his eyes narrowing with contempt. "Because from where I'm sitting, you've come out of it quite well. Two dead husbands, and you're sitting in a multi-million pound house, about to collect a fortune in life insurance. I decided your story needed professional scrutiny."

'This is my home," I say, a flash of genuine anger breaking through my performance. "And that money is what I'm left with. It's what David would have wanted."

"David would have wanted to be alive!" Robert snaps, leaning forward, his voice tight. He jabs a finger at the envelope. "I hired someone. A private investigator. Just to look into things. To give me peace of mind."

The room tilts. A private investigator. I had not accounted for this. A meddling, grieving brother acting outside the official channels of the police - a rogue variable of pure, emotional malice.

"What did he find?" I ask, my mouth dry, forcing the question out.

"Nothing conclusive," Robert admits, but his eyes gleam with a predatory light. "Not yet. But he found enough to make me question everything. He found out about the increased life insurance policy David took out six months before he died. He found rumors about your affair with Mark starting long before you claimed. And he found a witness, an old woman who lives opposite your old apartment, who says she saw a woman matching your description leaving the night David died. Not in the morning. In the night."

The old woman. Edith Higgins. I remember her. A curtain-twitcher I had dismissed as insignificant. A fatal error born of overconfidence.

"It wasn't me," I say, the lie automatic. "She must be mistaken. I was at my sister's. We had a movie night."

"That's your story," Robert says, picking up the envelope and tapping it against his knee. "And you've stuck to it. But stories can change. And evidence has a way of turning up." He stands up, looking down at me with pure contempt. "This isn't over, Chloe. The police may have closed the case, but I haven't. I will find out what you did to my brother, and I will make sure you don't keep a penny of that money."

He turns and walks out, leaving the door open, the sound of the rain pouring in, a cold, violent noise.

I sit frozen on the sofa, the carefully constructed walls of my new life cracking around me. I had neutralized the state. I had outmaneuvered a seasoned detective. But I had not anticipated the wild card of a brother's love. A new, nonsystematic problem has entered the game. And he is not playing by any rules I understand.

CHAPTER 39

NOW

The sound of Robert's car fading down the wet street is swallowed by the drumming rain. I remain on the sofa, paralyzed, the echo of his threats ringing in the silent, spacious house. A private investigator. A witness. The insurance policy.

Fool. I have been a proud, arrogant fool. I was so focused on the grand chess match with Detective Rossi, on outsmarting the official machinery of justice, that I failed to see the simpler, more direct threat of personal vengeance. Grief and greed are powerful motivators, and Robert is fueled by both.

He doesn't need forensic proof or a watertight case; he only needs enough suspicion to make my life a living hell, to tie up the insurance money in court for years, to stand up at the reading of the will and call me a murderess in a court of public opinion.

I cannot eliminate him. His death, so soon after this confrontation, would be a beacon pointing directly at me, confirming every single suspicion he harbored. He is not a loose end like Mark; he is a tripwire.

The rain intensifies, lashing against the windows. The storm outside mirrors the one now raging within me. My mind, usually a place of cool, clear strategy, is a chaos of panicked calculations. I need to discredit him, to make his vendetta look like the ravings of a bitter, jealous brother, unhappy with his inheritance and lost in grief.

But how? Attacking him directly will only lend credibility to his grief.

I think of the envelope. What else does his investigator have? He mentioned the insurance policy. I can explain that. David was becoming more cautious with age, it was his idea. The affair? Deny, deny, deny. It's his word against mine, and I am the grieving widow. But the witness... the old woman across the street. That is a problem. Memory is fallible, but a jury loves a credible witness.

I need to create a distraction so powerful that it redirects his entire focus. He needs a new villain.

A plan begins to form, dark and desperate. It's not elegant. It's not the masterful psychological manipulation I prefer. It is blunt and cruel, relying on the predictable intensity of his fraternal love. But it is all I have.

I need to give Robert a new phantom to chase, a figure so compelling he abandons his pursuit of me entirely. I need to weaponize David's reputation, to suggest secrets in his past that made him a target for a powerful, shadowy force.

I stand up, my legs shaky. The passive resistance is over. The time for waiting has passed. Robert has forced my hand. While Rossi is distracted by the ghost of James, I must deal with the very real, very angry ghost of David's brother.

I walk to the window and watch the rain-soaked street. Robert's visit was a declaration of war. And I have just decided on my first counter-attack: feeding him the ultimate lie to ensure he never looks back at me.

CHAPTER 40

THEN

There is a hierarchy of problems, and understanding this hierarchy is crucial to survival.

At the bottom are the minor inconveniences - a blocked drain, a rude shop assistant, a husband who questions your spending. These are solved with simple, direct action: a plumber, a sharp retort, a carefully deployed tear. They require minimal calculation and pose no existential threat.

Then there are the strategic problems - a marriage that has become a cage, a lover who has outlived his usefulness, a detective who is too perceptive. These require extensive planning, finesse, a deep understanding of human psychology, and often involve multiple steps and players. They are complex puzzles, and solving them is my art form. I treated James, David, Mark, and Sarah as strategic problems.

But at the top, the most dangerous kind of problem is the emotional one. The one driven not by logic or greed, but by raw, messy forces like love, grief, and a sense of injustice. Robert is an emotional problem. He is a bull in a china shop, and he does not care about the destruction he causes to my carefully constructed life. You cannot reason with a bull. You cannot manipulate it with a subtle gesture of vulnerability or a cold threat. He is deaf to strategy.

You can only redirect its charge. Or you can put it down.

Robert cannot be put down; his death would immediately confirm his suspicions. So, I must redirect him. I must make him charge in a different direction, towards a target of my choosing. I need to give him a new, more compelling reason for his brother's death - a truth that will eclipse his current theory of my guilt.

I think of the information I have. The life insurance policy. What if Robert believed David was in trouble? What if he believed David had taken out that policy because he was being threatened by a dangerous, outside force? What if I could plant evidence suggesting David had secrets - gambling debts, an affair of his own, some shady business dealing - something that would make him a target for someone other than me?

It would reframe the entire narrative. Robert's anger would shift from me, the widow, to the shadowy forces he believes destroyed his brother. He would cease to be an accuser in my tragedy and become an ally in a larger, more complex tragedy.

It is a risk. It means fabricating another layer to an already complex lie. It means expanding the scope of the deception to include David's fictional flaws. But it is a better option than trying to discredit a grieving brother directly. The world has sympathy for a grieving brother. It has less for a man chasing a phantom, especially a phantom I provide for him.

The plan is taking shape. I will create a phantom for Robert to chase, a target that can consume his time, resources, and emotional energy far away from my front door.

CHAPTER 41

NOW

The following day, the rain has cleared, leaving the world washed clean and bright - an ironic contrast to the filth I am about to generate. The hypocrisy of it is almost amusing. I put on my most respectable outfit - a tailored navy dress, somber but elegant - and drive to a branch of my bank in a city an hour away, ensuring the transaction has no traceable connection to my immediate location.

I need a safe deposit box. And I need to create a document that will shatter Robert's current belief system.

Inside the sterile, quiet room, I lay out my tools. A cheap, disposable pen purchased anonymously. Several sheets of generic typing paper I purchased from a different store. And the most dangerous item: a flash drive containing a scanned copy of David's signature, obtained from old digital contracts on his computer before I erased the drive.

Using a small, portable light tablet I brought with me, I carefully trace David's signature onto the bottom of a sheet of paper. It's not perfect, but it will pass a casual inspection by a man desperate for answers. Then, I begin to write the body of the note. I use a stilted, anxious tone, trying to channel how a man like David - private, controlling, and terrified - might write if he were cornered.

"I don't know who to trust. The calls are getting more frequent. They know about the money. They said if I don't pay by the end of the month, they'll go to the police about the Amsterdam incident. I had to take out the policy. It's the only way to get the cash together without raising flags. If anything happens to me, it's them. It's not Chloe. She doesn't know anything. Keep this safe. -D"

The "Amsterdam incident" is a complete fabrication, a vague enough reference to suggest a business misdeed or a personal scandal involving a large sum of money. It is a brilliant, open-ended hook - something for Robert and his investigator to waste their time and resources chasing across Europe. It absolves me entirely and provides a clear motive for David's death and the timing of the insurance policy.

I fold the letter, place it in a blank envelope, and seal it. I don't address it to Robert. I simply write "TO BE OPENED IN THE EVENT OF MY DEATH" on the front, lending it an air of final urgency. Then I place it in the safe deposit box, along with a few inconsequential pieces of David's old jewelry to make it look like a genuine repository for his secrets.

The key to the box is the final piece. I drive to a quiet park on the outskirts of my old neighborhood, the one where David and I used to walk on Sundays. I find a bench we often sat on, and I tape the key securely to the underside of it, hidden in the shadows of the iron frame.

The stage is set.

Now, I need the anonymous tip. Not to the police this time, but directly to Robert. Another email from a burner account, sent from a library computer in yet another town. Short and simple, preying on his grief.

"Your brother was scared before he died. He left something for you. Look under the bench in Queen's Park, the one by the old oak. He wanted you to know the truth."

I send the email and erase the history. As I drive home, I feel a strange emptiness. This is not the clean, surgical work I am proud of. This is messy. It relies on too many variables, on Robert's grief making him credulous. But it is the only move I have left.

I have created a ghost for Robert to chase. I only hope it is a convincing enough phantom to lead him away from my door forever.

CHAPTER 42

NOW

The wait is shorter this time. Robert is a man possessed, and the bait I dangled was too tantalizing to ignore.

Two days after I sent the email, my doorbell rings again. He stands on the porch, but the aggressive posture is gone. He looks haggard, confused, the rigid certainty he had before now fractured by doubt and complexity. In his hand, he holds the envelope from the safe deposit box, slightly crumpled.

"Chloe," he says, and his voice is different. Softer. Laced with a bewildered pain that speaks volumes of his internal struggle. "We need to talk."

I let him in, my expression one of cautious concern and manufactured fragility. "Robert? What's wrong? You look terrible." He doesn't sit. He just holds up the envelope, a sacred relic now. "I found this. A tip. An anonymous email led me to a key, and the key led me to a safe deposit box. This was inside."

I take the envelope from him, my hands trembling with a performance of nervous confusion. I make a show of reading the forged note, my eyes widening, my free hand coming to my mouth in shock. "My God... David wrote this? What... what is the 'Amsterdam incident'? Who was threatening him?" The questions pour out of me, perfectly pitched between shock and a dawning, horrified understanding.

"I don't know," Robert admits, his shoulders slumping. He runs a hand over his face in defeat. "I didn't know about any of this. He never said a word. He was being blackmailed, and he never came to me." The hurt in his voice is genuine. I have successfully redirected his anger away from me and towards the shadowy "them."

"This... this changes everything," I whisper, sinking onto the sofa as if my legs can no longer hold me. I look up at him, my eyes glistening with manufactured tears. "All this time... I thought it was a random break-in, followed by Mark's terrible guilt. But he was targeted. He was murdered because of this blackmail." I let a sob catch in my throat, a sound of profound relief and tragedy. "Oh, David..."

The transformation in Robert is complete. The accuser has become the ally. He sits beside me, his anger now a shared grief. "I'm sorry, Chloe," he says, his voice rough with emotion, reaching out a hesitant hand to touch my shoulder.

"I'm sorry I accused you. I just... I couldn't understand it. It didn't make sense."

"I know," I say, placing a comforting hand on his arm, sealing the alliance. "I didn't understand either. But now... now we have a direction. We have to find out who did this to him, Robert. We have to find them."

He nods, his jaw set with a new determination. "We will. I'll have my investigator look into this. Amsterdam... business contacts... we'll find them. They won't get away with it."

He leaves shortly after, the forged note carefully tucked back into the envelope, a sacred text now guiding his quest for justice. I close the door behind him and lean against it, the energy draining from my body, leaving me hollowed out.

It worked. The phantom has taken solid form in his mind.

But as I stand there in the silence of my hall, a new, more insidious thought slithers into my mind. I have just created another narrative, another layer of lies. And lies, no matter how well-crafted, have a way of intersecting. What happens when Robert's investigation into the fictional "Amsterdam incident" collides with Rossi's investigation into the fictional James Sterling/Anna Clarke connection?

I have built two separate fictions to contain two separate threats. But the world is not that neat. Stories have a tendency to bleed into one another. And I am the only person standing at the bloody crossroads.

CHAPTER 43

THEN

I used to believe that control was about building walls. Impenetrable barriers between the different versions of myself, between the truth and the lies I lived.

The version of me with James was a carefully constructed ideal - adventurous, carefree. With David, I was a masterpiece of submissive manipulation - fragile, dependent. With Mark, I was a desperate soul seeking salvation - righteous, passionate. And now, for the world, I am the tragic widow, victimized by fate and the cruelty of anonymous blackmailers. I built a wall around each life, each identity, believing that if they were kept separate, they could not contaminate each other.

But I was wrong.

Control is not about building walls. It is about managing the flow between them. It is about being the master of the sluice gates, deciding which truths and which lies are released, and when. A wall, when it cracks, collapses catastrophically. But a managed flow can adapt, can redirect pressure, can absorb shocks.

The confrontation with Robert taught me that. I could not wall him out; his grief was a flood that would have broken down any barrier I built. So I redirected him. I opened a new channel - the Amsterdam fiction - and let his anger flow in a direction of my choosing.

But now, I have two powerful, self-sustaining flows to manage: Rossi's pursuit of justice (chasing James/Anna), and Robert's quest for the truth (chasing Amsterdam blackmailers). I have opened channels for both, but they are now running parallel to each other.

My fear is that they will find a point of confluence. A single, inconsistent detail - a timestamp that doesn't match, a name that appears in both fictions, a financial record that leads down two different paths - could cause the channels to merge into a torrent that will sweep me away. Robert's PI will be looking at David's phone records for contacts; Rossi's team will be doing the same. What if they find the same inconsistency?

I am no longer a builder of walls. I am a water engineer, desperately trying to control two raging rivers with only my wits and my willingness to sacrifice anything - and anyone - to keep them from meeting. My carefully constructed reality is one accidental data point away from complete structural failure.

CHAPTER 44

NOW

The confluence happens sooner than I could have ever feared.

A week passes in a tense, fragile peace. Robert calls once to update me - his investigator is making "promising" leads in Amsterdam, following the money from David's business. I make encouraging noises, my stomach a knot of anxiety. Detective Rossi does not call. I take this as a good sign; she is deep in the past, exhuming James's reputation.

Then, on a Tuesday afternoon, my personal phone rings. It's not Robert. It's not Rossi. It's my sister, Emily.

Her voice is shrill, panicked, barely recognizable. "Chloe, there are police at my house! They're asking about you! About the night David died!"

The floor drops out from under me. "What? Why? What are they asking?"

"They're asking if I'm sure you were here all night! They're saying there's a... a discrepancy. Something about your mobile phone data showing it was active near your old house that night!"

The mobile phone. Another blind spot. In my focus on staging the scene, on creating alibis and forging notes, I forgot the digital leash in my pocket. I was so careful to leave my phone at my sister's during David's murder, but I must have turned it on briefly, just for a moment, to check the time, to send a single signal to Mark... a single, stupid, fatal mistake. A ping from a cell tower that places me at the scene.

"Just tell them I was with you," I say, my voice tight, the command sharp. "Stick to the story, Emily. It's a mistake. A technical error."

I hang up, my heart hammering a violent, frantic rhythm. This is it. This is the point where the rivers meet. Rossi's investigation, with its forensic precision, has collided with the timeline of my alibi. The mobile data is a crack in the foundation of my entire story.

And I know, with a sickening certainty, who gave her that specific thread to pull. Robert.

In his newfound, zealous investigation into David's "blackmailers," he would have had his own investigator pull all of David's records - phone, financial, everything. And in doing so, he would have seen the same records. He would have seen the ping from my phone near the apartment that night. And in his desire to find the "truth," he would have taken this discrepancy not as evidence of my guilt, but as proof that the "real killers" were active in the area, perhaps even framing me. He would have gone straight to Rossi with it, a gift, a piece of the puzzle that links all the disparate elements.

His attempt to help has doomed me. The walls are not just cracking. They are crumbling. The two narratives I so carefully constructed are collapsing into each other, and in the wreckage, the only clear figure standing is me.

I have run out of phantoms to create. I have run out of channels to redirect. The truth is exposed.

There is only one move left: flight.

CHAPTER 45

NOW

The world narrows to a single, burning point: escape. The meticulous life I built is collapsing around me, and the fire is spreading too fast to contain. Rossi has the phone data. It's only a matter of hours, perhaps minutes, before she connects it to the rest - the staged suicide, the forged note to Robert, the entire house of cards. I can't outmaneuver digital evidence. I can't redirect a cell tower ping.

I move with a frantic, yet controlled, energy. This is not the calm calculation of before; this is the desperate, primal flight of a cornered animal. I go to the safe hidden behind a false wall in the walk-in closet. I keep a "go-bag" there -

passport, cash in multiple currencies, a second untraceable phone, the essentials for a complete disappearance. I had always considered it a paranoid fantasy, a concession to the fear I denied. Now, it is my only reality.

I stuff a few more items of clothing and non-traceable jewelry into a small, expensive-looking suitcase. I must look like a wealthy widow going on a spontaneous trip, not a fugitive fleeing justice. My hands are shaking as I zip the bag closed, the sound loud in the silent house. I need to get to the airport. I have enough cash for a one-way ticket to a country with no extradition treaty - somewhere far, where I can disappear and reinvent myself again. It's what I'm best at.

I take one last look around the bedroom, at the pristine, empty space that was supposed to be my final, perfect victory. It feels like a museum exhibit of a life that never really was.

As I turn to leave, my personal phone rings. The screen flashes: Detective Rossi.

My blood turns to ice. She's calling. Not coming. That's something. It means she might not have an arrest warrant yet. She might still be building the case, trying to draw me out. This is a test. A final probe.

I let it ring three times, forcing myself to breathe, to slow my racing heart. I must sound normal. I must sound like a confused, grieving woman, not someone on the verge of flight.

I answer. "Detective?" My voice is impressively steady, laced with just a hint of weary confusion. "Mrs. Sterling." Her voice is flat, devoid of its earlier tiredness or frustration. It is the voice of a hunter who has finally cornered her prey.

"We need you to come down to the station."

"The station? Whatever for? Has there been a development with that Sarah woman?" I ask, playing my part to the end.

"We've received some new information regarding the night your husband, David, died. There are some inconsistencies with your statement that we need to clarify."

"Inconsistencies? I don't understand. I was at my sister's. I told you everything."

"The phone records suggest otherwise, Mrs. Sterling." The words are delivered like hammer blows, precise and devastating. "Your mobile phone was active on a cell tower less than a mile from your old apartment at 11:04 p.m. that night."

I am silent, my mind racing for a plausible lie, but the well is dry. There is nothing. "There... there must be some mistake," I stammer, the genuine fear in my voice now impossible to distinguish from performance.

"That's what we need to clarify. In person. Please come to the station within the hour." It is not a request. It is an order.

"I... I will," I whisper.

The line goes dead.

I stand in the hallway, the suitcase at my feet. I have a choice. I can go to the station and try to talk my way out of this, to spin one more brilliant, desperate lie. But I see the certainty in Rossi's voice. She knows. Going to the station means walking into a cell. Or I can run. Now.

I look at the suitcase. Then I look at the door. The game is over. It's time to disappear.

CHAPTER 46

NOW

The drive to the airport is a blur of rain-smeared streetlights and frantic calculations. Every police car I see is a potential threat, every glance from another driver feels accusatory. I am a ghost already, passing through a world that is no longer mine. The world has moved on, but the past is catching up.

I park my car in the long-term lot, abandoning it without a second thought. It is just a thing, a prop in a life I am shedding. I walk into the bustling terminal, a wave of noise and light and humanity washing over me. For a moment, I feel a pang of something - not regret, but a profound sense of dislocation. This is not the quiet, controlled exit I had imagined.

I head for the international departures desk, my eyes scanning the boards for the next flight out, anywhere. Rio. Bangkok. Nairobi. It doesn't matter. I just need to be gone.

I join a queue, my head down, trying to make myself small and unremarkable. I can feel the weight of the cash in my bag, my ticket to oblivion. I am three people from the counter. Two. My passport is clutched in my hand, the crisp pages separating me from my future.

"Chloe Sterling?"

The voice is quiet, but it cuts through the airport din like a scalpel, perfectly amplified to reach only me.

I freeze. I don't turn around. I know that voice.

Slowly, I turn. Detective Rossi stands there, flanked by two uniformed officers. Her expression is not triumphant. It is grim, resolute. She holds up a warrant.

"How..." is the only word I can manage, the failure absolute.

"The alert on your passport was triggered the moment you booked a ticket," she says simply, her voice low and efficient. "You can't run from your own digital footprint, Chloe. Not in this world. Not when you've moved millions through the system."

The world shrinks to the cold, hard reality of the handcuffs she places on my wrists. The metal is shockingly cold, a physical manifestation of my final capture. The other travelers stare, a sea of anonymous, horrified faces. I am no longer a ghost. I am a spectacle.

As they lead me away, I catch my reflection in a polished shop window. I see a pale; well-dressed woman being escorted by police. I look nothing like a master manipulator, a killer. I look like what I was always supposed to be: a victim. The irony is so perfect, so brutal, I almost smile.

CHAPTER 47

THEN

They say your life flashes before your eyes when you die. As the police car drives away from the airport, my life doesn't flash. It unscrolls like a blueprint.

I see the squirrel, stiff in the grass. My father's empty closet. James, disappearing beneath the dark water. David, lying on the floor. Mark, staring at me with hollow eyes. Sarah, weeping as they led her away. Robert, holding the forged note with desperate hope.

I see not the emotions, but the architecture. The cause and effect. The problem and the solution.

I built my entire life on a single, foundational principle: that I was the architect of my own destiny. That through intelligence and will, I could design my reality and eliminate any obstacle.

But a blueprint is not the building. And I failed to account for the weather. For the rot in the foundations. For the other architects - the Rossis, the Roberts - with their own plans, their own wills, and their own blind spots.

I thought I was playing a game of chess, a contained battle of wits on a fixed board. But the world was playing a game of entropy. And entropy, in the end, always wins. The more complex the system, the more inevitable its collapse. My masterpiece was too complicated to withstand a single, simple truth: a cell phone ping. My arrest is not a moment of justice; it is the natural consequence of mathematical failure.

CHAPTER 48

NOW

The interrogation room is a small, grey box. It smells of stale coffee and desperation. Detective Rossi sits across from me, the recording device between us a silent, blinking witness.

She doesn't yell. She doesn't threaten. She simply lays it out, piece by piece, like a path of stones leading to a cliff's edge, allowing me to see the futility of resistance.

First, the simple facts: The phone record, provided by Robert's investigator. The financial forensics linking the payments for the burner phones to an account I controlled. The testimony from the old woman, Edith Higgins, who, when re-interviewed with new context, was absolutely certain it was me she saw. The inconsistencies in Mark's "suicide" that her team had quietly continued to investigate. The absolute lack of any evidence for the "Amsterdam incident" or the mysterious blackmailers Robert was chasing.

Then, she plays her final, most devastating card.

"We exhumed James Sterling's body this morning," she says, her eyes locked on mine. "A strange request, I know. But given the new information linking him to the Anna Clarke case, a judge agreed. The post-mortem is ongoing, but the initial finding is... interesting."

I say nothing. I keep my face a perfect, cold mask.

"The injury to his head," Rossi continues, her voice unwavering. "The one that supposedly knocked him unconscious before he drowned. The coroner says the angle and force are inconsistent with a swinging boom. They are, however, perfectly consistent with being struck by a hard, blunt object. Held in someone's hand."

She leans forward, her voice dropping to a near whisper, a final assertion of her victory. "Three husbands, Chloe. All dead. All in 'accidents.' How long did you think you could keep playing this game without the corpses whispering?"

I look past her, at the grey wall. I think of the lake. Of the storm. Of the poker in my hand. I think of the perfect, resonant silence after each one. The depth of her investigation, spanning three separate crimes across years, is staggering.

I look back at her, and for the first time, I let her see the real me. Not the victim. Not the grieving widow. The architect.

"You're right, Detective," I say, my voice clear and calm, devoid of all emotion. "It was a game." I lean forward, a small, cold smile touching my lips, acknowledging her victory. "And I was winning until you changed the rules."

CHAPTER 49

NOW

They put me in a holding cell. The door clangs shut with a finality that echoes in the sterile, tiled space. The air is cold, smelling of disinfectant and despair. This is not part of any blueprint I ever drew. This is the chaos after the collapse, the messy, uncalculated reality of containment.

I sit on the hard, narrow bunk, the thin mattress offering no comfort. I run through the interrogation again in my mind. Rossi was thorough. She has the phone record, the financial forensics linking the payments for the burner phones to an account I controlled. The testimony from the old woman, Edith Higgins, is subjective but compelling. It is a strong case.

But it is circumstantial. They have no murder weapon for David. They have no direct proof I killed James, only the suggestive autopsy report. Mark's death is the strongest, but even that relies on disproving the suicide narrative I so carefully built and proving the angle of the blow was homicidal.

A cold, sharp sliver of hope wedges itself into my mind. They need a confession. Without it, a skilled barrister could pick the case apart. Create reasonable doubt. I am a wealthy, respectable white woman. The world is predisposed to see me as a victim, not a predator. I can still win this.

The game has just moved to a new, more public arena - the courtroom.

The cell door opens and a uniformed officer gestures for me to stand. "Solicitor's here."

They lead me to a private room where a man in an impeccably tailored suit waits. He is in his fifties, with sharp, intelligent eyes and an air of unshakable calm, radiating competence. He introduces himself as Alistair Finch. I recognize the name - one of the most expensive, most ruthless criminal defense barristers in the country, known for his relentless, cynical efficiency. Robert must have hired him in his latest, desperate attempt to secure justice for his brother. The irony is almost beautiful; my enemy's ally has become my most valuable tool.

"Mrs. Sterling," he says, his voice a low, confident rumble. "Let's not waste time. The evidence is problematic, but not insurmountable. You will listen to me, and you will do exactly as I say. Your freedom depends on it."

For the first time since the airport, I feel a sense of equilibrium returning. I am back on familiar ground. Strategy. Leverage. A new player has entered the game, and he is entirely on my side, motivated by the challenge and the fee.

"Tell me what to do," I say, meeting his gaze with renewed focus.

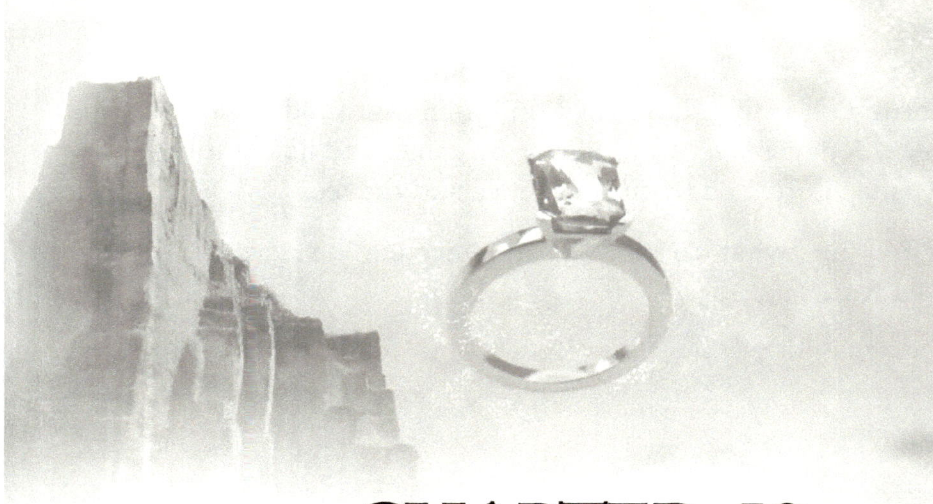

CHAPTER 50

THEN

My father's voice is a ghost in my ear. "Identify the problem. Find the most efficient solution."

The problem is the Crown's case - a scattered narrative of circumstantial evidence, two dead men, and one very unsympathetic widow. The solution is Alistair Finch and his ability to dismantle the case, piece by cynical piece.

Alistair Finch is the ultimate tool for this. He is a master of the legal battlefield, prioritizing victory over truth. His plan is not to prove my innocence, but to prove the prosecution cannot prove my guilt beyond a reasonable doubt.

He will attack the phone record - a single ping is not proof of presence, he will argue; the cell network is notoriously unreliable, capable of errors. He will destroy Edith Higgins's credibility - an elderly woman with poor eyesight, her memory manipulated by a grieving brother's vendetta, influenced by photographs she was shown. He will present Mark as a mentally unstable man, capable of staging his own suicide and framing me out of a twisted sense of guilt or revenge. He will argue that the financial links are coincidental, that I am a wealthy woman with many financial streams, easily misrepresented by police tunnel vision.

As for James and David, he will lean into the tragedy. He will paint me as a woman uniquely cursed, who loved men who met tragic ends. He will use the public's sympathy as a shield, ensuring the jury sees the victim the media created, not the killer Rossi captured.

It is a brutal, cynical, and brilliant strategy. It requires me to play the part I know best: the victim. The poor, unfortunate widow, relentlessly targeted by those who envy her wealth and pity her fate.

It is the most efficient solution available.

But as I listen to him lay out the plan, I feel a strange hollowness. This is survival, but it is not victory. Victory was the silent house, the freedom, the power. This is just... noise. It is the messy, loud process of legal defense, a compromise with the chaos I fought so hard to control.

CHAPTER 51

NOW

The media circus begins immediately. My face is splashed across every newspaper and screen. "THE BLACK WIDOW." "THE WIDOW'S GAME." They have even used the title of my unwritten novel. The irony is a private joke that sustains me in the long, empty hours in my remand cell.

Alistair Finch is a machine. He files motions, attacks the evidence, and manipulates the press with the skill of a puppeteer. He has managed to get the charges regarding James's death dropped entirely - there simply isn't enough evidence to move past the accidental death ruling, despite the suggestive autopsy. The focus is now squarely on David and Mark, the homicides directly tied to the cell phone data.

The trial date is set. I am moved to a remand centre, a purgatory of routine and waiting. My world has shrunk to this: a small room, legal documents, and the unwavering belief of my barrister that we can win.

One afternoon, I am called to the visitor's room. I expect it to be Alistair to discuss a motion. But it is not.

Detective Rossi sits on the other side of the thick, smudged glass. She looks tired, but her gaze is as sharp as ever. This is not a formal interview; it is a final, personal confrontation.

"Mrs. Sterling," she says, picking up the phone receiver.

"Detective. To what do I owe the pleasure? I thought we were done talking until we meet in court."

"I'm not here for pleasure," she says, her voice low and direct. "I'm here to give you a choice."

"A choice?" I mimic, my hand resting lightly on the cold plastic receiver.

"The trial will be a spectacle. It will tear apart what's left of your life, and the lives of everyone connected to you. Robert. Sarah Jenkins's family. Your sister," she lists them with cold precision. "And at the end of it, with the phone evidence and the angle of the blow on Mark, you will likely go to prison for a very, very long time. Your life will be reduced to a number and a concrete cell."

She lets the words hang in the air between us, allowing the grim weight of the consequences to settle.

"Or," she continues, leaning slightly closer to the glass,

"you can end it now. You can confess. A full, detailed confession for the record. In return, the Crown will accept a plea of diminished responsibility. You'll be sent to a secure psychiatric hospital, not a prison. It's a... cleaner ending for all involved."

I almost laugh. A psychiatric hospital? She still wants to fit me into a box, to explain me away as mad, not bad. She cannot comprehend the cold, logical calculus that has governed my life. She seeks a reason outside of pure, rational malice.

"You think I'm insane, Detective?" I ask, my voice quiet, laced with genuine curiosity at her fundamental misreading of me.

"I think you're a woman who made a series of monstrous choices," she replies, refusing to be drawn into the psychological debate. "The 'why' is for the doctors to figure out. My job is to close the case, and secure a measure of justice."

I look at her through the smudged glass. This is her final move. An appeal to a humanity she believes is buried deep within me. She is offering me a way out that preserves her worldview - that people like me are broken, not evil. She has not understood a single thing about me.

"I have a barrister, Detective," I say, my voice flat. "I'll see you in court. I do not admit to flaws in my design."

I hang up the phone and stand, turning my back on her before she can respond. The game is not over. There is still one more move to make on the board. And I intend to make it from the witness stand.

CHAPTER 52

NOW

The trial is a theater of the absurd, and I am the lead actress in a role I did not write, but one I have mastered. The courtroom is all dark wood and solemn faces, a stark contrast to the sensationalist headlines that scream my name. I sit in the dock, a placid expression on my face, wearing a simple, modest, high-collared dress chosen by Alistair to project innocence and vulnerability.

The prosecution presents its case. It is a relentless march of facts and figures - the phone records, the financial trails, the tearful testimony of my sister, Emily, who now looks at me as if I am a stranger. Robert sits rigid in the public gallery, his face a mask of conflicted pain, still clinging to the phantom of the Amsterdam blackmailers even as the evidence against me mounts.

Then, they call Edith Higgins. The old woman from across the street. She is frail, guided to the stand, but her voice is clear and sharp as a tack.

"That's her," she says, pointing a bony finger directly at me across the courtroom. Her eyes are not those of a confused old woman. They are clear and certain. "I saw her leave that night. It was raining. She had a dark coat on, and she looked... determined. Not scared. I remember because I thought it was odd, a woman leaving so late in a storm."

Alistair rises for cross-examination, his tone gentle, almost paternal. "Mrs. Higgins, you are how old?"

"Eighty-two," she states firmly.

"And your eyesight? You wear glasses, do you not?"

"I wear glasses for reading. My distance is fine."

"And the street was poorly lit, was it not? And it was raining heavily, obscuring vision. You expect the court to believe you could positively identify my client from across a street in those chaotic conditions, at eleven o'clock at night?"

"I know what I saw," she insists, her voice gaining strength, trying to overpower the subtle doubt he's introducing. "It was her. I saw her face in the porch light."

It is a pivotal moment. The jury is listening intently, swayed by her certainty.

Alistair changes tack, moving to the weakness I provided him. "Mrs. Higgins, are you aware that Mrs. Sterling's brother-in-law, Robert Sterling, visited you several times at your home before you gave this definitive statement to the police?"

She hesitates, looking momentarily confused. "He did. He was looking for answers about his brother, David. He was very upset."

"And during these visits, Mrs. Higgins, did he suggest to you what you might have seen? Did he, perhaps, show you a photograph of my client and ask if it was her you saw that night, to help jog your memory?"

The old woman's confidence wavers. "He... he might have. He was very upset, and he said he just wanted the truth."

"So, is it possible," Alistair says, his voice dropping to a conspiratorial whisper the jury must lean in to hear, "that the image in your mind, the face you are so certain of, was implanted there by a grieving man desperate for someone to blame for his profound loss?"

"I... I know what I saw," she repeats, but the conviction is gone, replaced by a flicker of doubt and fatigue.

Alistair sits down, a barely perceptible smile on his lips. He has done his job. He has introduced reasonable doubt by weaponizing Robert's grief.

I look at Edith Higgins, at the confusion on her face, and I feel nothing. She is not a person to me. She is a variable that has been successfully managed, dismissed not by my action, but by the legal system's required skepticism.

CHAPTER 53

NOW

The case for the defense begins. Alistair is a maestro, orchestrating a symphony of doubt. He does not call many witnesses. His strategy is to pick apart the prosecution's case, not to build one of his own, focusing the jury's attention entirely on the cracks in the state's foundation.

He calls a telecommunications expert who testifies about the potential inaccuracy of single cell tower pings, explaining how the data is suggestive, not conclusive. He calls a psychologist who speaks eloquently about the fragility of memory, especially when influenced by external suggestion and media pressure.

He paints Mark as the true culprit - a volatile, guilty man. Presenting evidence of Mark's own financial troubles and his possessive nature, Alistair suggests that Mark killed David in a fit of rage when his demands for money were refused, and then, consumed by guilt and paranoia, staged his own suicide to look like murder, framing me in the process as a final act of twisted revenge against the woman he believed rejected him.

It is a monstrous thing to do to a dead man, twisting his despair into final malice, but it is devastatingly effective. I can see the jury following the logic, their faces thoughtful, seduced by the narrative of a simple, tragic villain.

Then, it is my turn. Alistair advises strongly against it. "You are not a sympathetic witness, Chloe," he says bluntly, his professionalism cutting through the tension. "Your calmness will be read as coldness. Your intelligence as cunning. Let the doubt stand."

But I insist. This is my final performance. My last chance to look the world in the eye and show them the masterpiece I have created - a narrative so compelling it subsumes all others.

I take the stand. I swear to tell the truth. The courtroom is utterly silent, waiting for the Black Widow to speak.

The prosecution's barrister is a bulldog of a man. He goes straight for the jugular, dismissing the subtle doubt Alistair has seeded.

"Mrs. Sterling, you have now lost three husbands. Do you consider yourself unlucky?"

"I consider myself tragic," I reply, my voice soft but clear, ensuring every juror hears the word. I look at the jury, letting them see the sorrow in my eyes. It is a technically perfect performance, practiced over years.

He scoffs. "Tragic? Or convenient? Each of their deaths resulted in you receiving a significant financial windfall, did it not?"

"Money is a poor consolation for losing the person you love," I say, the lie flowing smoothly, tinged with a delicate, controlled indignation.

He bombards me with questions, trying to trip me up on timelines, on financial details. But I have lived this story for months. I am the author. I do not stumble.

Then, he asks the question I have been waiting for, the summation of their entire case.

"Mrs. Sterling, the prosecution contends that you are a highly intelligent, highly manipulative woman who planned and executed the murders of two men for personal gain. What do you say to that, now, under oath?"

I pause. I look directly at the jury, then at Rossi, who sits at the prosecution table, her expression unreadable, waiting for the final truth.

"I say that if I were the cold, calculating killer you portray me to be," I say, my voice dropping to a whisper that forces everyone to listen, "then I would have been much, much smarter. I would never have been so careless as to take my phone with me. I would never have chosen a lover so weak he would break under pressure and write a suicidal confession. I would have created a story so watertight that no detective, no matter how determined, could ever have found a crack."

I lean forward slightly, my gaze sweeping over them, offering them the final, irresistible truth.

"The truth is far simpler, and far more tragic. I am a woman who loved men who were flawed. Men who had enemies. Men who made bad decisions. And I am left alone to pay the price for their mistakes, stalked by a detective and accused by a grieving brother."

I sit back. The courtroom is silent. I have not confessed. I have done something more powerful. I have given them a narrative that is more compelling than the prosecution's clumsy tale of a black widow. I have given them tragedy. And the world understands tragedy.

I have just played my final, winning move.

CHAPTER 54

NOW

The jury is out for three days. The wait is its own form of torture, a slow drip of uncertainty. Alistair is cautiously optimistic, spending the time polishing the edges of our narrative. "You were brilliant on the stand," he says. "You gave them a story they can believe. Juries don't want to believe a nice, middle-class woman is a serial killer. They want to believe in tragedy, and you gave them the perfect tragic victim."

When we are called back into court, the air is so thick with tension it is hard to breathe. The court clerk stands, a piece of paper in her hand.

"Will the foreman of the jury please stand."

A middle-aged man in a cheap suit rises, his face carefully blank.

"On the count of the murder of David Sterling, how do you find the defendant?"

"Not guilty."

A gasp ripples through the room.

"On the count of the murder of Mark Greenwood, how do you find the defendant?"

"Not guilty."

The world seems to explode in a cacophony of sound - shouts, cries, the gavel banging relentlessly. Robert Sterling lets out a raw, anguished cry of betrayal and disbelief. Detective Rossi simply stares at me, her face a stone mask of defeat, her professional life's obsession rendered moot by twelve ordinary people.

I do not react. I do not smile. I simply turn to Alistair.

"Told you," he says, a genuine, relieved smile on his face for the first time.

I am free.

As I walk out of the Old Bailey, a free woman, the flashbulbs pop like a thousand tiny stars. Reporters scream questions. The public gawks. I am a celebrity, a notorious figure, but a free one. I have won. I have beaten the system. I have outsmarted them all.

I get into the waiting black car Alistair has arranged. As it pulls away from the chaos, I look out the window at the passing city. I have everything I wanted. My freedom. My money. My life.

And yet, as the car carries me towards my empty, silent house, the victory feels like ash in my mouth. I won the game. But the prize is a life lived entirely in a cage of my own making. A cage where every face I see is a potential accuser, where every relationship is a potential threat, where my only companion is the ghost of the women I killed. The perfect, resonant silence I craved is now my eternal sentence.

CHAPTER 55

NOW

Freedom is a gilded cage. The house, which once represented my ultimate victory, now feels like a museum dedicated to my own crimes. Every room holds a ghost. The kitchen where I poured Mark's drugged Scotch. The staircase where I staged the break-in. The bedroom where I ended him. The air is thick with the residue of my actions.

The public fascination is relentless. For a few weeks, I am the most famous woman in Britain. "The Black Widow Who Walked." My face is on magazine covers, my story dissected on daytime television. Alistair Finch manages the media with a deft hand, positioning me as a tragic figure vindicated by the courts, a woman ready to retreat from the world and heal.

He arranges a single, highly controlled television interview. I sit in a soft chair, bathed in kind light, and speak in a halting, soft voice about my grief, my shock, my desire for privacy. I talk about the toll the baseless accusations have taken on my mental health. I am flawless. The host's eyes well with sympathetic tears. The public, ever fickle, begins to shift its sentiment. From monster to martyr.

Behind the performance, the real work begins. The financial work. With the legal cloud lifted, the life insurance policies for both David and Mark are finally paid out. It is a staggering sum of money - a lifetime of comfort purchased by three deaths and two successful cover-ups. I spend days with accountants and wealth managers, a cold, bureaucratic process that feels like the final severance from the men who earned it. The money is no longer a representation of their lives; it is simply a number on a screen, a tool for my future. Whatever that may be.

I receive a letter. It is from Robert. It contains no salutation, no signature. Just one line, typed on a plain sheet of paper.

I know you did it.

It should frighten me. But it doesn't. It feels like an epitaph, a final, impotent acknowledgement of defeat. He is powerless now. The law has spoken. His knowledge is a burden only he must carry. I burn the letter in the kitchen sink, watching the paper curl and blacken into nothing. Another ghost laid to rest.

But one ghost remains more persistent than the others. Detective Rossi. Her silence is a threat, her absence a form of surveillance.

CHAPTER 56

NOW

She comes to see me a month after the trial. I am in the garden, pretending to tend to the roses, enjoying the scent of the living world. I see her walking up the path, and a strange calm settles over me. I knew she would come. This was the final, inevitable scene.

'Detective," I say, not looking up from a rose bush, snipping a dead head with detached precision. "Or is it just Maria now? Since you're no longer on my case."

"It's Detective Rossi," she says, her voice tight, formal. She doesn't have a warrant. She doesn't have any authority here. This is a personal visit, a final act of professional conscience.

I finally look at her. She looks older, the lines on her face deeper. The case has taken its toll; she lost. "To what do I owe the pleasure? A congratulatory visit?" I ask, my tone lightly mocking, unable to resist the final taunt.

"I'm here to give you a warning," she says. She doesn't try to come closer, to invade my space. She stands at the edge of the patio, a respectful distance away, but her presence is an invasion in itself.

"A warning? I'm a free woman, Detective. The jury saw the truth."

"The jury saw a performance," she counters, her eyes hard, unwavering. "I see you. I see the calculation in your eyes right now. You're not a grieving widow. You're a predator who got away with it, and you're enjoying the silence."

I smile, a small, cold thing. "Be careful, Detective. That sounds like slander."

"I don't care," she says, and the raw honesty in her voice is more disconcerting than any legal threat. "This isn't about the law anymore. This is about me and you. I'm telling you that I will be watching you. For the rest of your life, I will be watching. You will never apply for a job, you will never open a bank account, you will never take a trip abroad without me knowing about it. You may be free from prison, Chloe, but you will never be free from me. I will be the one constant in your perfect, boring life."

She turns to leave, then pauses, looking back at me over her shoulder. Her gaze is like a physical weight, a final pronouncement of her new sentence.

"Three husbands. That's a pattern. And patterns repeat. The next time you slip up, and you will slip up, I will be there. And I will not stop until you are in a cage, one that the court cannot open."

She walks away, leaving me standing alone in my perfect garden.

Her words should terrify me. But as I look around at the high fences, the silent, expensive house, I realize something. She's wrong. I am already in a cage. I just built it myself. Her surveillance is merely the lock I placed on the door.

CHAPTER 57

NOW

The world begins to forget. The news cycles move on to fresh scandals, new tragedies. The "Black Widow" becomes a footnote, a chilling story told in whispers at dinner parties. The reporters camped outside my door vanish, tired of waiting for the slip that never comes. The silence I once craved returns, but it is no longer peaceful. It is heavy, expectant. It is the silence of a stage after the play has ended, the audience gone home, leaving only the actor surrounded by empty seats and discarded props.

I try to find a new purpose. I consider philanthropy, donating large sums to charities supporting grieving widows.

The irony is not lost on me, and the idea feels like the ultimate performance, a joke only I can appreciate. I abandon it; the public gesture would only invite renewed scrutiny. I travel, using a fraction of my wealth to stay in luxurious, anonymous hotels across the globe - Paris, Tokyo, Dubai. But I am alone with my thoughts in every five-star suite, on every pristine beach. The scenery changes, but the prison of my mind remains.

I find myself drawn increasingly to the water. I rent a villa on a remote stretch of the Amalfi Coast, its terrace overlooking a vast, blue expanse that reminds me of the lake where James died, but on a grander, more indifferent scale. I stand there for hours, watching the waves, not with remorse, but with a strange sense of kinship with the element that was my first, perfect tool. Water is patient. It erodes. It waits. And in the end, it always wins against the rigid structures of the land.

One evening, sipping a bitter local liquor, I make a decision. I cannot live like this, a ghost in a gilded life. The game was the only thing that made me feel alive. The planning, the execution, the razor's edge between discovery and triumph. Without it, I have lost the only thing that gave my life meaning.

Rossi thinks she has sentenced me to a life of surveillance. She doesn't understand that she has given me a new opponent. A permanent one.

The game is not over. It has simply changed. The objective is no longer freedom or wealth. The objective is to outlast her. To live so flawlessly, so quietly, that her lifelong vigil becomes a monument to her own obsession, not my guilt. I will become so boring that I will erode her will, as the sea erodes the cliff. It is a game of endurance, and I have nothing but time and the cold, unshakeable will to win.

CHAPTER 58

NOW

A year passes. Then two. I become a master of banality. I establish a routine so mundane it would defy the scrutiny of even the most dedicated watcher. I buy a small, unassuming cottage in the Cotswolds under a limited company, adding a layer of financial anonymity. I rarely visit. My primary residence is the large, empty house, which I maintain as a stage, a symbol of the life I am supposed to be living - the wealthy, tragic, and utterly harmless widow.

I take up gardening in earnest. Not the decorative puttering of before, but a serious, almost academic study of soil composition, pruning techniques, and pest control. The garden is a new, controlled environment. I join a local horticultural society under my own name, attending monthly meetings where I speak knowledgeably about rose blight and the benefits of companion planting. I am polite, reserved, and utterly unremarkable. The other members see a quiet, wealthy widow with a green thumb. They have no idea that the woman deadheading her peonies is capable of deadheading a human life with the same clinical precision.

I know I am being watched. I feel it. Sometimes it's a car parked too long down the lane. Sometimes it's a new face in the village pub, a person who doesn't quite fit the local color. Rossi is making good on her promise. Her obsession is a cold comfort to me. It is proof that I still matter. That the game is still on.

I even send her a Christmas card one year, posting it from a distant city. A simple, tasteful card with a picture of a snow-covered landscape. I sign it, "Wishing you peace and quiet this holiday season. - Chloe Sterling." I don't know if she receives it, or if she understands the mockery in the sentiment. But it pleases me to send it. It is a move on the board, a subtle reminder that I know she is there, and that I am not afraid.

I am cultivating more than just a garden. I am cultivating a legend of normalcy so deep and so wide that it will bury the truth forever. I will become the most boring woman in England. And in that careful construction, I will find my protection.

CHAPTER 59

NOW

The third year of my self-imposed exile brings a strange, settled rhythm. My life has become a series of small, deliberate actions. I wake at seven. I take my tea in the solarium, reading the newspaper from front to back, not for the news, but to maintain the appearance of a person engaged with the world. I work in the garden for precisely two hours, often timing myself. I prepare myself a simple lunch. In the afternoons, I might drive to a nearby market or visit a local stately home, always alone, always polite and unassuming.

I have become a fixture. The quiet woman from the big house. I am known well enough to be greeted, but not well enough to be known deeply. It is a perfect equilibrium of presence and privacy.

One Tuesday, a new woman joins the horticultural society. Her name is Eleanor, and she has recently moved to the area. She is in her late fifties, sharp-eyed and intelligent, with a no-nonsense manner I find oddly refreshing. She sits next to me during a lecture on composting and makes a wry comment about the speaker's zealous passion for worm castings. I offer a small, genuine smile - the first true, uncalculated smile I've deployed in months.

We fall into a tentative, easy acquaintance. She is a retired librarian, she tells me. Widowed. She invites me for coffee at her cottage, a charming, cluttered place filled with books and the scent of old paper. We talk about literature, about gardening, about the slow pace of country life. It is the most normal interaction I have had in years.

For a few hours, sitting in her cozy living room, I almost forget who I am. The performance falls away, and I am simply a woman having coffee with a potential friend. The weight of my secrets feels lighter, almost bearable.

But as I drive home, the familiar walls of my mind reassemble. Is this a test? Is Eleanor one of Rossi's? A more subtle, more insidious plant than the obvious watchers in the pub? The thought is paranoid, but paranoia has kept me alive. I dissect her every gesture, every question, looking for the tell, the hidden agenda.

I decide it doesn't matter. If she is a plant, then the

performance must continue, but at a level of genuine banality that even Rossi cannot fault. If she is genuine, then she is a tool. A useful part of the facade of normalcy. A piece of the legend I am building.

I accept her next invitation. And the one after that. We become a regular feature, the two quiet widows, having tea, discussing books. I learn the rhythm of her life, her likes and dislikes. I file it all away. Data.

It is a new kind of game. A game of intimacy without vulnerability. Of friendship without trust.

The weeks pass, and my paranoia deepens. I find myself performing even when utterly alone. I narrate my own actions in my head, as if for a surveillance log. See how I gently water the azaleas, showing nurturing devotion to life? Observe the mundane selection of a ripe avocado at the market, evidencing a preoccupation with simple daily routines. Note the quiet, unassuming life I lead, entirely devoid of the high-stakes risk that once defined me.

During one of our afternoon teas, Eleanor notices. "You seem a bit distant lately, Chloe," she remarks, stirring a spoonful of honey into her Earl Grey. We are in her cottage, and a gentle rain patters against the windows. "You're usually so precise, but today you seem... frayed. Is everything alright?"

It is a simple, caring question. The kind a friend asks. I look at her - the fine lines around her eyes, the practical cut of her grey hair, the seemingly genuine concern in her expression. The doubt is the most potent weapon. Is this the masterpiece of Rossi's career? To find an actress so perfect, so utterly believable - a retired librarian with a fondness for composting

- that she could fool even me, the master of deception? Or is she simply a lonely woman who has found a companion?

The stakes of this judgment are immense. If I trust her, I risk exposure; if I reject her, I ruin the perfect facade of my new life.

"I'm fine," I say, offering a practiced, weary smile. "Just a bit tired. I haven't been sleeping well. The quiet takes some getting used to."

"Bad dreams, I suppose?" she asks, her head tilted, her gaze probing with a soft, natural curiosity that feels more dangerous than a direct interrogation.

"You could say that," I reply, and take a sip of my tea, letting the profound, unspoken truth hang between us. Yes, Eleanor. I dream of dead husbands and a detective who won't let me rest. I dream of the price of freedom.

She reaches out and pats my hand, a spontaneous gesture of comfort. Her skin is warm. "This time of year," she says sympathetically. "The grey skies. It gets into your bones, doesn't it? You just need a strong cup of tea."

Her touch is brief, but it feels like a brand. A claim. Whether it is a claim of friendship or a claim of victory for Rossi, I cannot tell.

I realize, with a cold clarity, that this is the new battlefield. Not a courtroom, not a dark apartment with a poker in my hand. It is this. The gentle clink of teacups. The murmur of sympathetic words. The treacherous, quiet warmth of human connection. It is a battlefield for which I have no map, operating under rules I cannot calculate.

And I find, to my cold satisfaction - and my growing unease - that I am very, very good at this game of intimacy without vulnerability. Even as I wonder: if Eleanor is genuine, what does it say about me that I cannot stop playing?

CHAPTER 60

NOW

The letter arrives on a day of relentless, grey rain. It is not a bill or junk mail. It is a thick, cream-colored envelope, hand-addressed in a looping, elegant script I do not recognize. There is no return address.

A prickle of unease runs down my spine. Very few people have this address. Alistair Finch. My wealth manager. Eleanor. Anyone else would use a standard business envelope or email.

I take it to the kitchen table, slitting it open with a bone-handled letter knife. Inside is a single sheet of heavy, watermarked paper. The message is short, typed cleanly.

I know you think you've won. You haven't. You've just chosen a slower, more tedious form of losing.

The world may forget, but I will not. I am the keeper of your truth. And I am patient.

It is not signed. It doesn't need to be. Rossi.

This is different from her confrontational visit. That was a declaration of war, loud and public. This is something else. An intimate whisper across the miles. A reminder that in the vast, boring landscape of my new life, there is one person who sees the cracks. One person for whom I am not a boring widow, but the most fascinating puzzle of her career.

I should be angry. Or frightened by her continued obsession. Instead, I feel a perverse thrill. The game had been becoming too easy, the moves too routine. This letter is a challenge. A gauntlet thrown.

She thinks my life is a form of losing. She doesn't understand that for someone like me, a life without a challenge is the only true loss. Her continued obsession is my victory.

I read the letter once more, then carefully fold it and place it in the pocket of my trousers. I will not burn this one. I will keep it. A reminder that somewhere out there, in the grey rain, my most worthy opponent is waiting. And so long as she is waiting, I am still playing.

The warning Rossi sent manifests within weeks. The carefully constructed dam of normalcy begins springing leaks.

A local online news blog, the kind that traffics in village gossip and lost cat notices, runs a small, cheap piece. "Tragic Widow or Cunning Criminal? The Local Woman at the Heart of a National Mystery." It's nothing substantial - a rehashing of old news, a few quotes from "anonymous neighbors" who say I keep to myself.

But it's a pebble that starts an avalanche, a signal that the external world remembers.

A few days later, a tabloid journalist finds his way to my door, drawn by the internet frenzy. I see him through the window, a young man with a cheap suit and a hungry look, his phone held up, no doubt recording the sterile exterior of the house. I do not answer. He leaves a card wedged in the doorframe, a physical threat to my privacy.

That night, I receive a friend request on a dormant social media account from a name I don't recognize. The profile is sparse, new. I delete it. Another appears an hour later. The curious, hungry public is finding the threads I thought I had cut years ago.

The watching eyes multiply. The car down the lane is now a different one every day. I see a woman with a long-lens camera pretending to photograph birds in the field opposite my house, her movements clumsy, amateurish, but persistent.

What triggered this? Robert's possible book? A persistent tip from a "concerned citizen"? Or simply the cyclical nature of public fascination, turning its eye back to an old scandal when new ones prove boring? It doesn't matter. The effect is the same.

Rossi's letter was the warning shot. This is the invasion.

The game is accelerating beyond my controlled parameters. The quiet, patient war of attrition is over.

I stand at my kitchen window, watching the amateur photographer in the field, and I understand with perfect clarity: the "Boring Woman" persona is compromised. I need a new defense, a radical reset.

I need to disappear entirely. I need to be a ghost.

CHAPTER 61

NOW

Becoming a ghost requires more than just silence; it requires active erasure. The renewed media interest is a brushfire, and I must starve it of oxygen before it consumes everything. The house, the garden, the local society - all of it is now compromised.

I call Alistair Finch. His voice, once a source of strategic comfort, now carries a new, weary tension, a clear acknowledgment of the legal system's inability to control public perception.

"The vultures are circling again, Alistair. They're at the

door."

"I've seen," he says, the sound of a keyboard clicking in the background. "It was inevitable, Chloe. True crime is a hungry beast, and you are its prime meal. I'll have my people issue cease-and-desist letters to the most egregious outlets. We'll threaten libel. It usually makes them back off from outright fabrication, but it won't stop the speculation, and it won't stop the amateur stalkers."

"It's not just the speculation," I say, my voice low as I stare out the window at the empty field where the paparazzi hid. "It's the feeling. The eyes. They're back, and they are multiplying. I am losing my ability to operate anonymously."

There is a long pause on the other end of the line. "Chloe," he says, his tone shifting from lawyerly to almost personal, a rare breach of his professional veneer. "You need to be prepared. This... scrutiny. It's your life now. You achieved the remarkable - an acquittal. But that doesn't grant you oblivion. It makes you a permanent figure of fascination, a cultural touchstone of ambiguity. You need to find a way to make peace with that, or you'll break."

Make peace with it. The words are so absurd I almost laugh out loud. Peace is the one thing my nature will not allow. The only states I understand are war and victory. And this, this constant, low-grade siege, is a form of war that favors the aggressor.

"Just do what you can, Alistair," I say, and hang up before he can offer further, useless counsel.

I look around my beautiful, sterile home. It is no longer a sanctuary. It is the most famous building in the village, a landmark of infamy. I cannot stay here. The "Boring Woman" of the Cotswolds is a persona that has been compromised and burned.

It is time for the final reinvention. Not a new character, but the absence of one. It is time to vanish entirely, to escape the physical and digital footprint of Chloe Sterling.

# CHAPTER 62

NOW

The plan for the final escape is complex and requires moving parts I haven't used in years, demanding a level of logistical precision usually reserved for covert operations. I spend a week in a state of focused, silent activity, a predator preparing its den for hibernation. The emotional toll of the prolonged surveillance has been entirely replaced by the focused concentration required for the mechanics of disappearance.

I use the second, untraceable phone, the one I'd kept for a true emergency - a necessary redundancy in my self-imposed security protocols. I call in a favor from a shadowy, discreet contact from a life I'd tried to leave behind - a man who specializes in new identities for people who need to disappear not just from the law, but from the relentless curiosity of the public and the media.

The new identity is a Dutch national named "Elise Visser." This persona is meticulously crafted: a woman of independent means, quiet, a lover of art and solitude. The paperwork is flawless, a masterpiece of bureaucratic forgery that can withstand preliminary scrutiny. The backstory is sparse - a recent inheritance, a desire for quiet retirement - designed to be uninteresting enough to resist a deep dive. The point is not to be utterly invisible, but to be geographically and historically disconnected from the notoriety of Chloe Sterling.

I begin the slow, careful process of liquidating portable assets. Not the major real estate or large investment funds - that would raise immediate flags with Alistair Finch's oversight - but the highly portable wealth. Jewels are sold to a discreet dealer in Antwerp through a series of intermediaries, funds moved through a labyrinth of shell companies over several weeks. Their final destination is a numbered account in Switzerland, accessible only to "Elise," providing a final, secure financial foundation.

I pack a single suitcase with clothes that are expensive but utterly unmemorable, in muted, neutral colours - the uniform of cultivated anonymity. I take no photographs. No mementos. The past is a country I am permanently emigrating from; every physical memory is a potential weakness. I scrub the house clean, leaving no personal residue, ensuring the 'Boring Widow' persona's departure is ambiguous.

I write a letter to Eleanor. It is the hardest part, the final, messy emotional variable I must deal with personally. I craft it with care, a masterpiece of benign deception. I tell her a distant, elderly relative in Canada has fallen ill, and I must go to care for her indefinitely. I apologize for the suddenness. I thank her for her friendship, noting its unexpected comfort. I use the word "bittersweet" to convey a sense of regretful duty. The lie is so much kinder than the truth.

I post the letter from a town forty miles away, using a remote post box. As I drop it in the box, I feel a strange, hollow sensation. It is not guilt. It is the feeling of closing a book mid-chapter, knowing you will never learn how it ends, severing the last thread of connection to my latest persona.

On my last night in the house, I walk through every room. I do not feel nostalgia. I take inventory. I see the ghosts, but they are faint now, like stains on a carpet that has been professionally cleaned. I have scrubbed away the emotional residue until only the facts of their deaths remain. Problems that were solved.

I am not leaving because I am afraid of being caught by the police. I am leaving because I have won the game I was playing here, and the board has grown stale. It is time to find a new one, one free of the physical constraints of my infamy.

CHAPTER 63

NOW

I become Elise Visser in a rented flat in Rotterdam. The space is modern, anonymous, filled with light from the canals and devoid of history. I furnish it simply, buying a few pieces of mid-century furniture and several large, abstract paintings. It is the home of a person with taste but no past.

My days are even quieter than before. I visit museums, walking slowly through the halls for hours, not truly seeing the art but absorbing the anonymity of the crowd. I sit in cafes near the harbour, a single woman with a book, indistinguishable from a thousand others. I am a leaf on a great river, moving without a sound.

For the first month, it works. The silence is a balm. The constant, performative pressure of being Chloe Sterling evaporates entirely. I sleep deeply, dreamlessly. I feel the rigid set of my shoulders begin to soften, the constant tension easing.

But the mind is its own country, and I am its only citizen. And in the quiet, the citizens of my past begin to hold their parliament.

James visits me first. Not as a ghost, but as a memory of a specific, sensory sensation: the sun on my face as we sailed, the way he would hum off-key when he was concentrating. The memories are not accompanied by guilt, but by a strange, aching sense of a door closing forever. The door to the person I was when I was with him - the ambitious, youthful version.

David comes next. I dream of the precise, metallic sound of his key in the lock of our old apartment. In the dream, I am waiting for him, but I don't know if I am going to kiss him or kill him. The line has blurred entirely. He was my project, my masterpiece, and now he is just a source of funds in a Swiss bank.

Mark is the most persistent. I feel his panic - it echoes my own, the raw terror I never allow to surface. The terror of a plan unraveling. I wake in the night, my heart pounding, the sound of the fireplace poker connecting with his skull as vivid as if it happened moments ago.

I have escaped the world, but I have brought my own, personal hell with me. It is a hell of perfect recall.

CHAPTER 64

NOW

The email arrives two months into my new life. It is sent to an encrypted, secure service "Elise" uses only for banking correspondence. Only one other person has the complex, secure address: my shadowy contact who arranged the new identity.

The subject line is blank. The body contains a single, carefully coded sentence.

The gardener is asking after the black roses. He says they are not thriving in this soil.

It is a code. A pre-arranged warning from my contact, using the terms we established. "The gardener" is Rossi. "Black roses" is me - a unique, artificially created thing. "This soil" is the Netherlands.

She has found me.

The shock is not one of fear, but of sheer, professional disbelief. How? I was meticulous. I am a ghost. I have no digital footprint under the name Elise Visser.

And then I understand. She didn't find Elise Visser. She never stopped watching Chloe Sterling. She wouldn't have chased the identity; she would have placed a tracker on my original assets, my passports, my financial structure. She would have had alerts set for any large, unusual financial activity from anyone connected to me - the liquidation of my jewels and the transfer of funds to the Swiss account.

She predicted my most logical move - that I would use my wealth to fund my disappearance. She didn't need to follow me; she simply waited for me to move the money.

She has been playing chess, thinking ten moves ahead. I thought I was free. She simply tipped over the board.

I close the laptop. The sterile, sunlit flat suddenly feels like a glass box. I am on display. She is out there, somewhere in this ancient city, and she knows my precise location.

She is giving me this warning not out of kindness, but as a final, devastating move. A demonstration of her absolute control. She is telling me that no matter how far I run, no matter who I become, I will always be her subject.

The game was never about putting me in a physical

prison. It was about proving that my mind, my freedom, my very self, is a territory she has already annexed.

CHAPTER 65

NOW

I book a flight. Not under a false name, but my own: Chloe Sterling. I use my own passport. I pay with my own credit card, ensuring the transaction is logged and transparent. I am done with hiding behind the flimsy constructs of anonymity. This is a deliberate, open act of resignation.

The flight is to England. I do not go to my elaborate, staged house in the Cotswolds; that home is a museum dedicated to the crimes I have chosen to abandon. I take a train from the airport, avoiding the rental car agencies, and then a taxi, instructing the driver to take me to a small coastal town in Norfolk.

It is a place of windswept beaches and vast, empty skies. The end of the land. A place where the land simply stops and yields to the sea. It is a physical embodiment of the emotional terminus I have reached.

I rent a cottage near the shore. It is small, damp, and smells strongly of salt and mildew - the pervasive odor of decay and persistence. It is the antithesis of every beautiful, controlled space I have ever inhabited. I do not decorate it. I do not try to impose my order. I let the chaos of the sea and the relentless weather in, accepting the lack of human control.

I know they will find me. It doesn't take long. On the third day, I see the car parked at the end of the lane. It is a plain, dark sedan, not attempting to be subtle. It is just there. A fact of my existence.

A week later, there is a distinct, low knock on the door. I open it, recognizing the precise cadence of the rap - three sharp sounds that are less a request and more a command.

Detective Rossi stands there. She is alone, eschewing the support of uniformed officers. She wears a plain coat against the coastal chill. She doesn't look triumphant. She looks tired, and older than I remember, the stress of her long obsession etched into her features.

"Chloe Sterling," she says. It is not a question; it is a statement of identity, a final acknowledgment of the truth.

"Detective Rossi," I reply, stepping back to invite her inside. "Would you like to come in? The kettle's just boiled. I imagine you've had a long drive."

She hesitates, visibly thrown by the ordinariness of the invitation, the lack of resistance, the simple offer of tea. Then she nods, accepting the terms of this final, non-legal meeting, and steps inside, carrying the cold, analytical air of the outside world with her.

CHAPTER 66

NOW

We sit in the small, cluttered living room, the furniture mismatched and worn. I pour tea into two mismatched mugs. The wind rattles the windowpanes, and the distant cry of a gull cuts through the small space. It is the first time we have been together without the formal, rigid structures of the law between us - no interrogation room, no lawyers, no recording device. Just two women in a dusty room by the sea, facing the truth.

"Why here?" she asks, her eyes scanning the room, taking in the profound lack of curation - no books, no photographs, no personal touches. She sees the emptiness I have cultivated.

"It's the end of the line," I say, wrapping my hands around the warm mug. "There's nowhere else to go that matters."

"You could have kept running," she presses, trying to force me back into the narrative of the fugitive.

"To what end?" I counter, taking a sip of tea. "You would always be there. Or the idea of you. You proved that my mind is the boundary I cannot cross. The internal surveillance would be relentless, even if you stopped physically watching. It's the same thing as being caught."

She is silent for a moment, studying me, digesting the concession. "The email. You understood the code immediately."

"I did," I confirm. "It was a masterstroke. You didn't catch me with handcuffs. You made me understand that I was already caught. That the resources I used for my freedom were the very tools of my capture."

"So, what is this?" she asks, gesturing around the stark room with controlled frustration. "Surrender? A final confession?"

"No," I say, looking directly at her, ensuring she understands the distinction. "It's a resignation. I am resigning from the game entirely. The cost of maintaining the victory became greater than the prize."

She barks a short, humourless laugh, a sound of professional exhaustion. "You don't get to resign, Chloe. Three men are dead, and one woman is serving time for blackmail she was forced into. That game doesn't end until you are in a cell."

"And you put one woman in a cage for the rest of her life," I counter, my voice still calm, leveling the final accusation. "You just did it without bars. You're watching me now, in this sad little cottage, and you're wondering if it was worth it. All those years. All that obsession. For this."

Her face tightens; I have struck a nerve, aiming for the self-doubt that must plague her. "This was never about justice for you, was it, Maria?" I use her first name deliberately, forcing a final intimacy. "It was a puzzle. The hardest one of your career. And now it's solved. And you have nowhere to put all that focus. All that brilliant, terrible energy. You're as trapped as I am, bound to the case that defined you."

She stands up abruptly, her chair scraping against the floor. The brittle calm between us shatters. "You are a monster," she says, her voice low and shaking with a fury I have never heard from her, a break in her professional composure.

"I am what I am," I reply, not moving, accepting the label. "And you are what you are. A hunter with no more quarry. I wonder which of us is more lost, the one who found freedom in silence, or the one who found silence when the chase ended."

She turns and walks out, leaving the door open behind her, the sound of the wind and the distant crash of the waves filling the small room. I do not get up to close it. I simply sit, and listen to the sound of the end of the world.

CHAPTER 67

NOW

The open door lets in the cold, salt-tanged air. I sit until the light begins to fade, until the grey outside the window deepens to black. The cup of tea in front of me grows cold, a thin, discolored scum forming on its surface. Rossi's words hang in the room, no longer an accusation, but a description: Monster.

Is that what I am? The word implies a deviation from nature, a thing that should not be. But I feel like the most natural thing in the world. A force of entropy. A consumer of lives who refused the predictable role of the victim. The world is full of predators and prey; I simply refused the role I was assigned and chose the role of the efficient eliminator.

I stand, my joints stiff, and walk to the door. I close it, shutting out the wind and the sound of the sea. The silence inside is immediate and absolute, a profound lack of sound that is more unnerving than the storm.

This is my life now. This small, damp box at the edge of the world. No more games. No more masks. No more elegant solutions.

There is a terrifying freedom in it. For the first time in decades, there is no next move to plan. No performance to maintain. The audience has gone home, and the actor is finally, truly, alone, free of the perpetual anxiety of exposure.

I do not turn on the lights. I sit in the growing dark, and I let the memories come, unbidden and unedited. Not as ghosts, but as facts. James. David. Mark. Three problems. Three solutions.

And for the first time, I ask myself the question I have spent a lifetime avoiding: What was it all for?

The money is a number in a bank. The freedom is this cold cottage. The victory is a detective who looked at me with more pity than hatred.

There is no answer in the dark. Only the echo of the question.

CHAPTER 68

NOW

Detective Maria Rossi sits in her car, engine off, a half-mile from Chloe Sterling's cottage. The rain has started, a fine, cold drizzle that blurs the windscreen. She has been here for an hour, the engine ticking quietly as it cools.

She doesn't know why she came back.

The confrontation in the cottage plays on a loop in her mind. You're as trapped as I am.

She had dedicated years, sacrificed relationships, poured every ounce of her formidable will into building the case against Chloe Sterling. She had seen the truth where others saw tragedy. She had been the smartest person in every room, the one who saw the pattern in the chaos. And now, it's over. She won. She cornered her, not in a courtroom, but in a damp hovel by the sea, and proved her point with devastating finality.

So why does it feel like a loss?

Chloe was right. The obsession was the engine. Now it's gone, and the silence it left behind is deafening, a professional vacuum. The other cases on her desk seem trivial, mundane. She misses the sharp, clean focus of the hunt. She misses her worthy opponent.

She starts the car. The headlights cut two weak paths through the gloom. She has nowhere to go but home. To an empty house and a dog that needs walking. To a life that suddenly feels too large, and too quiet.

She has spent her life defining herself by the monsters she caught. Now, with the ultimate monster neutralized, she has to figure out who she is without them.

CHAPTER 69

NOW

The fire is lit. A small, meagre thing in the grate, but it pushes back the damp chill of the evening, providing a fragile barrier against the coastal cold. I sit in my chair, the one that faces the window, though there is nothing to see now but my own faint reflection in the black glass.

The painting of the stormy sea is on the mantel, the small watercolour capturing the energy I no longer possess. The book is in my lap, unread.

I think of nothing and everything. The memories are there, but they have no power anymore. They are exhibits in a museum that no one visits, curated and cataloged, but lifeless.

I have spent a lifetime believing that to be known was to be vulnerable. That to be loved was to be controlled. That the only path to power was through the absolute sovereignty of the self.

I have that now. Absolute sovereignty. Complete control over my environment and my actions.

And I have discovered that a kingdom of one is the loneliest country in the world. The victory is cold, sterile, and entirely unsatisfactory.

The clock on the wall ticks. The fire spits. The wind moans softly under the door. I close my eyes.

There is no victory. There is no defeat. There is only the long, slow, silent sound of a life, finally, running out.

EPILOGUE

SIX MONTHS LATER

The cottage had a new tenant. A writer from London, seeking solitude to finish a book - a predictable exchange of one form of exile for another. He found the place through a letting agent, charmed by its starkness and the low, relentless murmur of the sea, seeking quiet for his craft.

On a cold afternoon, while trying to light a stubborn fire in the damp grate, he moved the small watercolour painting from the mantelpiece. It had been left behind by the previous occupant, a quiet woman about whom the agent knew little, other than she paid promptly and departed without fuss.

As he lifted the painting, a single, folded sheet of paper, yellowed and fragile, fluttered from behind the frame and landed softly on the hearth.

Curious, he picked it up. It was not a letter. It was a list, written in a precise, unwavering hand, the pen strokes meticulous and controlled.

James - The Lake - Freedom

David - The Poker - Project

Mark - The Sedative - Liability

There were no dates. No explanations of method. Just three names, three objects, and three single-word reasons that defined the purpose of their destruction.

The writer stared at the list, a cold knot tightening in his stomach. He knew the story, of course. Everyone did. The Black Widow of the Cotswolds. He had even considered writing about her once, but the case was too cold, the ending too ambiguous for a satisfying book.

He looked around the small, damp room. This is where she had ended up. In this very chair, perhaps, staring at this same fire, consumed by her own creation.

He read the list again. It was not a confession designed for police. It was an inventory. A clinical, final accounting of a life's work, a summary of a meticulous career. It was a document of pure, chilling self-analysis.

He never did light the fire that night. He sat in the growing dark, the list held loosely in his hand, listening to the wind and the sea. He thought about the woman, and the three men, and the terrible, simple arithmetic of it all - the cold cost of absolute self-sovereignty.

In the morning, he took the list to the edge of the cliffs. The wind tore at his clothes, sharp and cold. For a long time, he stood there, the paper pinched between his fingers.

Then he opened his hand.

The wind snatched the list, carrying it out over the churning, grey water. It fluttered for a moment, a tiny, white scrap against the vastness of the sea and sky, before being swallowed by the waves.

He turned and walked back to the cottage. He did not know why he had done it. It was not evidence. It proved nothing in a legal sense.

But some stories, he thought, are not meant to be solved. They are only meant to be known. And then released, back into the silence from which they came.

ACKNOWLEDGEMENTS

Writing a novel is a solitary journey, but publishing it is a collective effort requiring immense dedication, expertise, and faith. I owe an immeasurable debt of gratitude to the people who helped transform this manuscript into a book.

First and foremost, I want to thank the incredible team at **MK Storyworks**. Your belief in *The Widow's Game* and your meticulous work were essential to its success. Thank you for your unwavering commitment and for guiding this project every step of the way. Your professionalism, attention to detail, and tireless effort in bringing my vision to life have been truly inspiring.

To my readers: Thank you for picking up this book. I hope it keeps you up all night, just as I intended.

And finally, to my family and friends—thank you for the patience, the endless supply of coffee, and the quiet support during the long days and nights spent chasing this story.

— F.M. Lock

A LETTER FROM F.M. LOCK

Dear readers and lovers of suspense,

I want to say a huge thank you for choosing to read **The Widow's Game**. Taking this journey into Chloe Sterling's world of meticulous planning and deadly secrets means the world to me. I truly hope it kept you up all night!

The truth is, writing is only half the adventure; connecting with you, the reader, is the other half! I love hearing from readers and seeing which twists resonated most—or which character you loved (or loved to hate!). You can easily get in touch with me through my publishers and their Facebook page: facebook.com/mkstoryworks.

Two Small Favors?

If you truly loved *The Widow's Game*, I would be incredibly grateful for two small favors that make a huge difference:

1. **Write a Review!** Your honest review on retailers like Amazon, Goodreads, or wherever you bought the book is gold. It helps new readers discover one of my books for the first time, and it truly fuels the creative process.

2. **Tell a Friend!** If you know someone who loves a fast-paced psychological thriller with a twist, please recommend *The Widow's Game*. Word of mouth is the best compliment an author can receive.

Ready for More? The Game Is Never Over...

If you finished *The Widow's Game* and felt Detective Rossi's job wasn't quite done, you're right. I'm thrilled to announce my next novel is **THE HUNTER'S DEBT**.

In this sequel, the silence has become unbearable for Detective Maria Rossi, three years after Chloe Sterling walked free. Rossi won the legal battle but lost the war: the debt of James Sterling's murder, disguised as an accident, fuels her obsession. The exhumation report—revealing blunt force trauma inconsistent with a swinging boom—is a truth she can't ignore.

The hunt begins anew when a piece of overlooked forensic evidence surfaces in the **Anna Clarke cold case**—the very case Chloe used to frame James. The new lead points not to James, but to someone still alive and connected to his past.

As Rossi gets dangerously close to the perfect vacuum Chloe has created in her exile, she realizes The Widow has already factored the detective's every move into her calculation. To catch Chloe this time, Rossi must risk everything, including the painful understanding that her life, like Chloe's, is **meaningless without the game.**

Stay Updated!

To keep up to date with **THE HUNTER'S DEBT** and all my latest releases from **MK Storyworks**, just sign up for the newsletter and updates through my great publishers: www.mkstoryworks.com

Thanks!

F.M. Lock

DON'T MISS THE ABSOLUTLEY EXPLOSIVE AND SHOCKING TWISTY SEQUEL TO THE WIDOW'S GAME

THE HUNTER'S DEBT
SNEAK PEEK

It's been three years since Detective Maria Rossi closed the book on Chloe Sterling, and the silence has been unbearable.

Rossi won the battle but lost the war: Chloe walks free, exiled to a cold, damp cottage by the sea. The police watch is routine, a bureaucratic gesture. But for Rossi, the surveillance is personal, fueled by the conviction that James Sterling—the first husband—was no accident. The memory of the exhumation report, the blunt force trauma inconsistent with a swinging boom, is a debt her conscience refuses to let her forget.

Now, a new lead surfaces in the old **Anna Clarke** cold case, the very case Chloe used to frame James years ago. A piece of forensic evidence, overlooked by the original team, points not to James, but to someone connected to his past—someone still very much alive.

The truth is a lure, and Rossi cannot resist the chase.

But as she digs into James's past—the man Chloe so meticulously crafted into a killer—Rossi finds herself getting dangerously close to the **perfect vacuum** Chloe has created in her exile. Rossi soon learns that The Widow is not only still capable of observation, but that she has already factored the detective's every move into her own calculation.

To catch Chloe this time, Rossi must risk everything: her badge, her sanity, and the painful understanding that her life, like Chloe's, is meaningless without the game.

The hunter must pay the price of her obsession.

The game is never over.

ABOUT THE PUBLISHER

MK Storyworks is a truly global book publisher, dedicated to the timeless mission of connecting compelling authors with enthusiastic readers across the world.

We pride ourselves on curating a diverse and dynamic list that spans the full spectrum of literary interests. Whether you are looking for an immersive escape into a bestselling fiction novel, seeking wisdom and knowledge from groundbreaking non-fiction titles, perfecting a dish with our acclaimed cookbooks, or introducing the magic of reading to the next generation with our enchanting children's books, MK Storyworks delivers stories that inform, entertain, and inspire.

Our commitment to quality, creativity, and global reach ensures that every book we publish finds its place in the hands and hearts of readers, no matter where they are.

Connect with MK Storyworks

Stay up-to-date with our latest releases, author news, and behind-the-scenes glimpses by connecting with us online:

Website: www.mkstoryworks.com

Social Media:

- YouTube: @mkstoryworks
- Instagram: @mkstoryworks
- Facebook: @mkstoryworks
- X: @mkstoryworks
- Pinterest: @mkstoryworks
- TikTok: @mkstoryworks